KERSTIN HENSEL

*TRANSLATED FROM THE
GERMAN BY JEN CALLEJA*

Peirene

Tanz
am Kanal

AUTHOR

Kerstin Hensel was born in 1961 in Karl-Marx-Stadt in former East Germany and studied in Leipzig. She has published over thirty books: novels, short-story collections, poetry and plays. She has won numerous prizes, including the Anna Seghers Prize, as well as the Lessing Prize for her entire body of work.

TRANSLATOR

Jen Calleja is a writer, literary translator from German, editor and musician. She has translated book-length works for Fitzcarraldo Editions and Bloomsbury, as well as short fiction, essays, articles and poetry. *Dance by the Canal* is her first book for Peirene.

MEIKE ZIERVOGEL
PEIRENE PRESS

When I pass homeless women, I look into their faces and wonder: why her and not me? I sense that maybe our differences are not as great as I would like to believe. *Dance by the Canal* tells the story of a woman who fails to find her place in society – neither in the communist GDR nor in the capitalist West. Her refusal to conform to the patriarchal structures of both societies forces her into ever-increasing isolation. This book will make you think.

First published in Great Britain in 2017 by
Peirene Press Ltd
17 Cheverton Road
London N19 3BB
www.peirenepress.com

First published under the original German-language title *Tanz am Kanal*
Copyright © Suhrkamp Verlag Frankfurt am Main 1994
All rights reserved by and controlled through Suhrkamp Verlag Berlin

This translation © Jennifer Calleja, 2017

Kerstin Hensel asserts her moral right to be identified as the author of this work in accordance with the Copyright, Designs and Patents Act 1988.

The translation of this work was supported by a grant from the Goethe-Institut, which is funded by the German Ministry of Foreign Affairs.

 GOETHE INSTITUT

ISBN 978-1-908670-38-0

Designed by Sacha Davison Lunt
Photographic Image by Don Baird / Getty Images
Typeset by Tetragon, London
Printed and bound by T J International, Padstow, Cornwall

KERSTIN HENSEL

TRANSLATED FROM THE
GERMAN BY JEN CALLEJA

Peirene

Dance by
the Canal

Now that I'm sitting down here by the left pillar of the bridge with this large, smooth sheet of packing paper at my feet, I feel joy for the first time in years. It's no coincidence that fate has brought me this paper – I've been chosen to write. I've been put on this earth for no other purpose than to tell the story of my life, and today I will begin.

Up on the bridge it's hot, a once-in-a-century July day. Air shimmers over the asphalt. Squinting up, I see silver and grey, car tyres, women's legs, men's legs, children, dogs. Up on the bridge life is sweating, the city is baking. Here, where I'm sitting, it's cool. The canal drifts serenely by. It's so hot that from time to time the water stops flowing, or changes direction, or becomes a thick mush. But it's cool under my bridge. I squat against the damp stone wall, my hair sticking to the back of my neck, water from the bridge soaking into my shirt. Dripstones and moss lurk in the dark vaults above me. Drops quiver on the tips of stalactites and don't fall for a long, long time, and then they splash onto the stony embankment, or onto my knees. Sometimes it can take days for a drop to fall from the deck of the bridge. The bridge is always damp, water is constantly seeping from its old stones. It's a good thing that I don't have to sweat like the people up in the city, it's a good thing that I'm not radiating heat like a car tyre, or having to rush to work, or hurry home thirsty.

I found a big sheet of blue packing paper and stole a dozen wooden pencils. It's pleasantly shady here, on this once-in-a-century July day in 1994 in the city of Leibnitz, where I'll begin to write the story of my life. A task I once hated and was coerced into doing has now become a need.

This desire to write has come from sitting under *my* bridge, the last free bridge in Leibnitz, the bridge I conquered. It's a desire that comes from having a place of my own. I make myself comfortable. My old jeans are protected by the three sheets of honeycomb board I'm sitting on. I don't have anything else, and this is as good a place as any to begin.

I'm writing under my real name: Gabriela von Haßlau. They used to call me Binka when they thought I was being stupid or silly, and Ehlchen when I was being a good girl. Gabriela only when they hated me. My earliest memory is of a violin case. I got it for my fifth birthday. Brown leather on the outside, green silk on the inside. I opened it and looked at the instrument and I thought it was an animal, an enchanted dachshund. I began to wail and my father pulled my braids.

– It's a violin!

Uncle Schorsch was visiting us from Saxony. He laughed.

– What a silly little Binka your daughter is!

Mother blushed. Father chanted in my face:

– Repeat after me! Vi-o-lin! Vi-o-lin!

I cried over the bewitched dachshund. Mother took it out of its case and placed it in my hands.

– Careful! said Father, and the violin bow stroked the dachshund's fur, which Father called strings.

– Repeat after me! Str-ings! he said.

As the dachshund whimpered, I cried like never before. Uncle Schorsch roared with laughter and sloshed cognac over his shirt.

– Let Ernst be earnest! Mother pleaded, trying to hush her brother.

Uncle Schorsch snorted behind his handkerchief.

On the evening of my fifth birthday, I held the violin in my left hand and the bow in my right. I scratched away and the violin made the sound of a cat screeching.

– F sharp! Father commanded, and: D sharp!

I curtsied, just like I'd been taught to. There was goose liver pâté on the table and Mozart on the record player. The villa rang out with music and smelled of birthdays. Uncle Schorsch was laughing and spilling whatever he could find on the dinner table down his shirt: cognac and Russian sparkling wine, pâté and salad. I learned to tell the difference between a dachshund and a violin. My father was a vascular surgeon. And even though it was my birthday, he still talked about varicosis. It was his favourite word, and I listened carefully whenever he pronounced it. I loved this word because I never had to repeat it. Va-ri-co-sis! was never asked of me.

It was my father's word. *Mine* were words like violin, pâté, Mozart. Uncle Schorsch's words were mine too: beddy-byes, stroppy madam, in a huff. Father forbade Uncle Schorsch's words.

– It's bad German, he said, and really, unless Uncle Schorsch can find something better than being deputy director of the Consumers' Cooperative Union in Grimma soon, then...

Mother tried to soothe her husband:

– Well, you can't choose your family.

– You can! Father said, and: Diction matters. Repeat after me, *diction*, Christiane!

Uncle Schorsch would leave of his own accord once his supply of laughter and jokes had run out. It was usually after the *Sandman* show. We owned a television and the time with the Sandman was mine. Ten minutes, and then I had sleeping sand in my eyes and Uncle Schorsch declared:

– Your peepers are teeny and your doggy is sleepy.

– Violin! Father shouted.

Uncle Schorsch said goodbye. And while I tried to sleep, Father and Mother argued in the living room. I pulled the bedcovers over my ears and whispered: Violin,

violin, violin. The next morning Father had already left for work at the clinic. The sun was shining through the villa's old, large windows. Mother dashed around trying to mop up dust. A dirty tablecloth and the last of the pâté were the only visible remains from the birthday party. The violin case lay brown and menacing on the cabinet in the living room.

– You ought to take lessons, Ehlchen, Mother said.

I couldn't go to kindergarten because Father was the chief vascular surgeon and Mother was a housewife. I couldn't play in the street either because there wasn't anything to do on our street. And anyway, the villa had a garden where I was allowed to draw a hopscotch court in the gravel with a stick. Father called it Heaven and Hell, Uncle Schorsch called it Hop Score. Bad German. I hopped from hell into heaven on my own, my left leg hitched up, my jumping leg too shaky to reach heaven unpunished: it landed on the dangerous lines, or next to the box, or would buckle completely. I fell by the wayside. I had no one to play against. Father made sure I didn't fall in with bad company. But I didn't have any company, good or bad. Underneath the stairs that led to the laundry room in the cellar at the back of the villa, spiders had spun their webs. They stayed hidden in the back part of their den, black and skulking. I collected ants and beetles for them, and sometimes, as a special treat, earthworms. I would place the tiny creatures on the edge of the web and the spider would pounce from its hiding place, killing the victims with a single bite before sucking them dry. I fed the spiders every day until Mother caught me, shredded the webs with the mop, and squashed each and every one of the little beasts.

I wore patent-leather shoes, tights, a petticoat, a cotton vest and a green and red crocheted dress. Or a blue and white crocheted dress. Mother plaited my black hair into French braids, which were held in place with golden bands. Before bed she would tear tangles out of my hair with a brush, pulling them out until I whimpered with pain.

– Think of all the people with varicose veins, Father would say, you don't see them crying.

Mother cried. She was sitting on the red plush sofa with a bottle of cognac in front of her, Father's favourite drink. Mother drank two or three cognacs and a siren wailed from inside her. She was like a stranger. I felt frightened and wanted to call Father at the clinic, but then the siren stopped and Mother said very quietly:

– They've shot your Uncle Schorsch.

The word *shot* wasn't one of my words, or Mother's, or Father's. It didn't belong to Uncle Schorsch either. It simply appeared, conjured out of nowhere. It sounded like bad German. I shook my head and whispered in Mother's ear:

– You're not allowed to tell anyone, it's our little secret, OK?

Mother nodded and pulled me onto her lap.

– You silly little Binka, she said, you have to forget all about Uncle Schorsch.

I promised I would. That evening Father turned the television up very loud and I heard it again, the word *shot*, and I heard other words too: showdown, peace. The siren wailed inside Mother. The Bad German in our family died with Uncle Schorsch. Father decided to find me a violin teacher. Frau Popiol wore a curly red wig and a pinstriped suit like a man. She brought her son Kurt, who was stupid. Cretin, Father said. Kurt crouched in the furthest corner of the music room. He was always shaking his head and bending his pale sausage fingers back against the joints. I watched the boy with interest. He was maybe fourteen years old and he fascinated me.

– Don't be frightened of Kurt, he's a sweetheart, Frau Popiol said.

I wasn't afraid of Kurt, it was his fingers that scared me, the way he bent them like rubber. Frau Popiol told me to stand in front of the piano and took the violin out of its brown case.

– What's this?

I didn't say anything because I knew that Frau Popiol knew that I knew. But Frau Popiol didn't back down.

– What is this?

– A doggy, I said.

Kurt clapped his hands.

– You're learning the violin, Frau Popiol said, and touched her red wig nervously.

– Vi-o-lin.

– Yes.

I obediently picked up the instrument and played F sharp, C sharp, D sharp.

– STOP! commanded the teacher. I dropped the bow.

– Pay attention, child.

– Yes.

– Do *you* want to learn the violin?

– Yes.

– Not everyone gets this opportunity.

– Yes.

– How old are you?

– Five.

– The right age.

– Yes.

– Do you know what a note is?

– Yes.

– Yes?

– Yes.

She showed me the correct way to hold the bow. Elbows out. Relax. Fingers loose. Straight back. Elbows out. Head bent to the left. Relax. Fingers loose. Elbows out. Not like that. Yes, like that. Higher. *Higher*.

The bow quivered. I just looked at Kurt, crouching happily and foolishly in the corner, a monkey, slobbering, shaking his head. I would have liked to know if he wanted to play the violin. For a second time the bow fell on the floor. Frau Popiol's hand rapped on the piano lid.

– What are you thinking about, girl?

– Vi-o-lin.

– Right, let's start by testing your rhythm. Copy me!

Frau Popiol clapped her hands, I copied her, and mis-clapped on the second beat.

– Hopeless, but your father's set on it.

– I want to play with Kurt.

– I'll come back again tomorrow. Then you'll know how to hold a bow.

Frau Popiol took me in her arms to say goodbye, kissed my braids, her red curls mixing with my black plaits. She kissed me for a long time, until she reached the base of my neck and I was shaking from the tickling. Kurt bent his fingers and Frau Popiol pulled him up out of his crouch and onto his feet.

– See you tomorrow, Ehlchen, she said.

Ehlchen was my mother's word.

The writing is going well. Steam is rising from the canal. Today Leibnitz's wool-dyeing factory flushed red into it, yesterday it was blue, blue like packing paper. After three hours of writing I take a break, raise myself up from my corrugated seat, stretch. I have to stay close to my bridge, otherwise the squatters might move in. I myself have attempted to squat twice before: I went under the Sunday Bridge and the Green Bridge looking for a place to sleep out of the wind. And both times, the cardboard already laid out and me covered with my grey blanket from the

shelter, their lordships showed up. Rat! That's our spot!
Three men, old canal dancers, mangy and randy. This,
they said, was *their* place. I didn't know, so I took my
blanket and cardboard and plastic bag of belongings. I
ran from the Sunday Bridge to the Green Bridge. This
was the one thing I knew from my first day of homeless-
ness back then: it was forbidden in doorways, gateways
and under balconies. So I headed for the Green Bridge,
which wasn't in the centre of Leibnitz and had only a
small sliver of an embankment. But the Green Bridge
was occupied too. And those pieces of shit chased me
away: Go to a hotel! They took my blanket and laughed
at me with their tooth stumps. Bet she's from the welfare office, piped up a young one, and the mob bleated,
mooed, brayed at me along the canal. You have to get
your own patch. Territory is territory. I learned quickly,
found *my* bridge, between the wool-dyeing factory and
the old industrial plant. It's just called the Canal Bridge
and holds off the wind and rain. Or the heat in once-in-
a-century summers.

Stiff from sitting, I stretch my limbs and step out
from under the bridge's shadow. Great to have written
so much. The world of my childhood matches the warm
rust red the canal is offering today. Summer shimmers
over Leibnitz. I'm free. Today, with the unstoppable
decline of my family completed, I realize that all of it
set me up for independence. Granted, I'm alone and
too scruffy to attract another person's attention in the

near future, but what is this disgust people have when they come across me, or the pity they cough up while sweating under their sense of obligation? As if things are better for them. No one knows my name any more, no one knows what I've done, who I was, who I am. What a stroke of luck. I have to admit that I'd see things differently if I hadn't been chosen to write. I would doss, drink and stink. But I don't stink. I'm clean. I wash every day in the water fountain in Schiller Park, early in the morning, when the gate's still closed. Then I eat breakfast at the shelter. Or I wash at the shelter and have breakfast in the park.

– Everything's fine, I say. But it's only fine because I can write.

By midday I'll have filled the whole reverse side of the packing paper. I feel the momentum within me, a heaving, driving pleasure.

I learned to play the violin. After two weeks of lessons, Frau Popiol was happy with the way I held the bow. For the first proper note I needed another two weeks. Kurt was the only one impressed by my playing. He flexed his fingers and grinned whenever his mother poured her own toxic brand of teacher's frustration over me. I was unmusical. Father paid Frau Popiol well. In May 1963 he was appointed chief medical officer at the surgical clinic. And on the day of his appointment he behaved like a normal human being for once. At breakfast he sat me on his knee. I could smell the Spike aftershave he'd received from his varicose vein patients from the West.

– Giddy up, rider! he sang, and the tips of his black moustache wiggled.

– Today is a big day, Ehlchen. Today I will become the chief medical officer.

Mother, too, was cheerful.

– You'll have to become even more earnest, Ernst.

– I have a surprise for you, Ehlchen.

Father lifted me into the air and kissed my mouth. His breath smelled like a pharmacy.

– Today you're going to play the violin for the doctors' collective.

He knocked back a cognac and left the house. I didn't want to. Refused. Frau Popiol was called in for crisis management and she beat out: F sharp! C sharp! D sharp! Until it stuck. Mother ironed a white lace blouse.

– Don't embarrass us, child.

– The child *will* embarrass you, Frau von Haßlau.

– What are we paying you for, Frau Popiol?

F sharp! C sharp! D sharp! The doggy howled, squeaked, whimpered.

– You're playing it *wrong*, Gabriela!

– But we're paying you, Frau Popiol.

The party at the surgical clinic drew closer. Chief Medical Officer Ernst von Haßlau collected Mother and me at the clinic door. He stood before me, large and white and smelling of unfamiliar cognac.

– Stay in the septic zone.

Septic was one of Father's words. I held the violin case under my arm and swallowed the word septic. Mother smiled nervously, hanging off her husband's arm. We walked through the reverberating hallways of the clinic, tight, high corridors where the paint was peeling from the ceilings in big patches. The old yellow on the walls reeked of lacerated knees that had been doused in antiseptic. The doors, lacquered white and with mysterious names written on them, like Laboratory, Ultrasound, Op I and Op II, were damaged and rotten. A whimpering sound was coming from somewhere, a metallic clatter from somewhere else.

– Keep up, Ehlchen. They're waiting for us.

I ran on tiptoes between my parents, the violin case dangling from my hand. I felt terrified, as if I was about to have a massive injection.

All I remember of the party is the blue hole. I was on a small stage with the violin in my hand, a room full of white figures in front of me. I lifted the bow – and fell into the blue hole. I woke up on a trolley, opened my eyes – above me was Father's moustache, quivering at the ends.

– Gabriela!

A nurse appeared and fed me some drops.

– Do I have varicose veins too? I asked.

There was laughter all around. But Father wasn't laughing.

– We are going to find you another teacher. I've been utterly humiliated. You'll be the death of me.

I lay on the trolley in Op II, the huge, round lamp above me. I hoped that it would come crashing down and bury me.

Bottles of cognac orbited above me. The doctors said a lot of words, none belonging to me.

Because they couldn't find anyone else, Frau Popiol remained my violin teacher. Father thought it over for many hours and came to the conclusion that Frau Popiol was strict enough, respectable enough and passionate enough to teach me the violin. But Kurt, who Father saw as a distraction, had to sit in the kitchen from then on. Mother fed him cake.

I was so unmusical that Frau Popiol gave up on me after a year of futile effort. In the final lesson I played 'Hänschen klein' almost faultlessly, and then the bow fell out of my hand. That's it. Frau Popiol tore the red flames from her head. Under her wig: gleaming white skin. The flames lay next to the violin bow. That's it. I closed my eyes and awaited my punishment.

– Come, Frau Popiol said.

– Vi-o-lin, I said.

Frau Popiol placed her hands over my closed eyes. I could smell resin, sheet music. The hands stroked down my nose and across my mouth, tenderly and awkwardly and slowly and endlessly. Frau Popiol's fingers opened my lips; sticky with fear, my lips offered resistance. The fingers pressed my upper and lower jaws apart. The violin teacher's fingers pressed through my gappy teeth.

– Come.

– Where?

– Wherever you want.

I swallowed, bit down. Ungifted. That's it. Frau Popiol laughed. Now my eyes were open. I stared at the bald head with fascination.

– Come!

A strange tongue on mine, a forceful strange tongue, thrusting and churning between my teeth, inside my little-girl mouth, wherever you want, Frau Popiol's tongue didn't stop, Frau Popiol's fingers didn't stop, the blue and white crocheted dress, I wanted to say something, sing something, unmusical, but you were paid well, come! Frau Popiol lifted me into the air. She was a strong, stunningly beautiful woman, I floated in her arms, flew from the distress, towards the bliss. That evening I told my parents about this bliss.

The violin was shut away in its case. The case was put away in the attic.

– Frau Popiol is sick, I heard Father say.

Varicose veins, I thought to myself. Father will make her better.

– No, once and for all, no.

I never had to have a violin lesson ever again. I started school that September.

*

I've filled the front and back of the packing paper. Strange how easily the words come to me. Have to maintain the flow. I just have to avoid falling down that last hole. That would mean the end of freedom. But where I'm at now, I'm nowhere near the end. Earned myself a meal. Can't leave the bridge. If the tramps come it's all over. But why would they come today of all days when they have the Sunday Bridge and the Green Bridge? My bundle of papers and my bag of things all tied together, I go to eat. There's fish in mustard sauce at the shelter, once a gymnasium named after Aviator Cosmonaut Sigmund Jähn. Excellent. And I receive a new blanket. The clothing steward remarks:

– Maybe you'd like to give a job or an apartment a go, Fräulein Haßlau?

– *Von* Haßlau, I correct her.

A pitying shake of the head. But I know who I am. Well fed. Summer. Once-in-a-century heat. Leibnitz is dozing. Most of the factories have closed down, most people are at home or who knows where. Maybe on holiday in the Canary Islands... The sun blinds me. I could go to Schiller Park and wander by the neatly trimmed bushes like a tourist. Or sleep on a smooth, white marble bench. Or wash my hands.

Schiller Park. At the fountain. Goldfish snapping at my fingers. My reflection shows straggly black hair. I should wash it. Tomorrow evening at the shelter.

You're not going to get me! I pull my fingers out of the fountain. They didn't catch me, not a chance. At the park's exit I find two cone-shaped paper bags, one with bright flecks of cherry juice on the edge, the other clean, smooth, as if new. Tearing them apart makes two semicircular sheets of paper, enough to keep writing.

Full and clean, I make my way back to my spot under the bridge. The coast is clear. All mine. The canal is still flowing rust red. The only brewery still open has discharged its waste water into it, hop brew mixes with colour, a cocktail for rats. I indulge myself in a little nap on the new blanket from the shelter before I continue writing. I wake up just as a drip falls from the largest stalactite and lands on my forehead.

I was called Gabriela *von* Haßlau.

Thirty first-year pupils laughed. Schneider-Dagmar, Grumert-Thomas, Gallwitz-Jutta and whatever their names were all laughed about something that Father and Mother never laughed about; about something that everyone at Father's clinic marvelled at in awe and pronounced with particular care: *fffon* Haßlau.

– Noble Anhaltinian stock, said Chief Medical Officer Ernst von Haßlau.

– A bourgeois relic, said our teacher Fräulein Brinkmann.

Back home I shrieked:

23

– They laugh about *von*, they laugh at me, I don't want to go to school, I don't want to be called *von*, no one else is called *von*, we're a *soshalist* school, we—

– So-cial-ist, Father corrected. Repeat after me.

I was stubborn. Didn't want *von*. Father summoned Fräulein Brinkmann and had words with her. The next day the class didn't say a word when Fräulein Brinkmann called out:

– Gabriela von Haßlau!

Even at that age I knew that she would leave me alone from then on because of Father. He was a doctor, a chief medical officer. The other children's parents were machinists, textile workers, clerks. Fräulein Brinkmann reminded me of a chicken: gaunt, featherless, with a saggy neck. Her voice seemed to come out of her ears, her mouth barely made a sound. She cheeped the multiplication tables and the alphabet, she cheeped while up against thirty-one rowdy children, her throat getting plumper, her body getting thinner. One day she couldn't say another thing and crumpled into her chair.

At night I dreamed of Frau Popiol. In my dreams she was our teacher. Anyone who managed to solve a difficult maths problem would be crowned by her red wig. I was ungifted and never received the wig, but there was nothing I wanted more than to possess those flames. So I sold my violin to Kurt in exchange for a magic powder that would make me the best at maths in the whole school. I solved every problem, but Frau Popiol kept her wig.

I cried and came up with more amazing solutions. But Frau Popiol shook her bare head.

– I'm sick, Gabriela, you know that.

– But the others...

– Yes, the others will soon lose all of their hair too, they need my help.

– Are they all sick?

– Yes, Gabriela. Frau Popiol laughed, cackled, and suddenly she looked like Fräulein Brinkmann.

– *You* made the children sick! I screamed.

– It was your father, said Frau Popiol.

I woke up, got out of bed and tottered into the living room. The light was still on. Father was sitting in his huge armchair drinking cognac, still wearing his suit. He'd already emptied half the bottle; long, thin shards of glass and cigarette ash lay all over the parquet floor. Father stood up unsteadily and shooed me out of the room.

– Get out of here.

– I had a bad dream.

– Get in bed with your mother.

I ran into the bedroom and lay beside Mother. In the morning, Father was asleep in his armchair, still wearing his suit. He'd overslept. An ambulance picked him up and took him to work. Mother poured the Napoléon cognac down the toilet. The whole bathroom smelled of it. She swept up the shards and the ash. She was a calm and placid woman; only when she swept and cleaned did a furious energy come over her. She would thrust the scrubbing brush into every corner, water splashing. She would press thick brown rolls of beeswax into the linoleum, rubbing them in with violent, circular motions, scooting around on her knees. The iron-weighted floor scrubber clicked and clacked, Mother yanking it this way and that, ten times over the same place, until the floor gleamed. She went over the parquet with the duster mop, and each time she shook it out of the window and dust clouded up she would groan:

– This filth, this perpetual filth!

On the windows she used Klarofix, blue ammonium chloride; for the toilet and washbasin Ata scouring powder; all day long she scrubbed and polished, pulling muscles in her knees and back. Father wanted to employ a cleaner, but apparently they didn't exist in socialist Leibnitz. So he brought home three nursing students. They buzzed around the villa with a broom and bucket, then received ten marks each. They were sworn to secrecy and told to return to the Herr Doktor's once a week. Soon certain items of jewellery went missing, along with imported soap and perfume. On International Women's Day I gave my mother an upholstered knee cushion that was covered with wax cloth.

I didn't get on at school. I couldn't figure out what they wanted from me. Fräulein Brinkmann, the chicken, sent me to sleep. I was always tired, whereas the other children babbled and clowned around and pelted Fräulein Brinkmann with staples.

– I expected more from a doctor's daughter, Fraulein Brinkmann said to me with a sad, helpless look.

– You're far more intelligent than all the others.

Or, to be more precise, there was a big red 'I' for 'Intelligentsia' next to my name in the register as a result of my father's occupation. Next to all the others were 'L' for 'Labourer' or 'C' for 'Clerk'. I could tell that Fräulein Brinkmann was alluding to this 'I' in an attempt to get through to me. She was looking for an ally.

– I can play the violin, I told her.

Fräulein Brinkmann smiled.

– Well, there you go. Then why don't you pay attention in class?

– Frau Popiol was better.

– And who is Frau Popiol!

– My teacher.

– *I* am your teacher.

I avoided Fräulein Brinkmann. I knew that I had to do something to not stand out. The 'I' was a sign in the register. From then on I did my fair share of staple throwing and chair rocking. My fellow pupils cheered me on and accepted me as one of them: Ha, the doctor's kid wants to play too!

Joining in was fun. It was a world away from playing hopscotch in the garden – a world full of rowdiness and thumping opened up to me, boisterous fun that could

27

be triggered by a despairing teacher. The Good German of my parents was far behind me and I wallowed in the other children's expressions. Most importantly of all, it brought me into the company of Katka Lorenz. Katka, the smallest, fattest and dirtiest among the girls in 1a. She had eight siblings, her mother worked doing laundry, and Katka didn't know her father. After school Katka took me back to her flat on Leninstraße: into a cradle of filth and slovenliness. I held my breath, went giddy from the stench and the allure of the place. Trousers, skirts, coats, underwear for ten people hanging, lying around, knotted together; mattresses and duvets an indistinguishable jumble; apples, a loaf of bread, beer bottles, baby rompers: a heady spell.

Katka showed me how to put on her big sister's clothes. She was an angel. Katka told me how her big sister would hit her and how she, Katka, would then kick her little brother. Katka showed me how to steal gobstoppers from the cooperative store. Katka was musical. She danced without music, she was always dancing, waltzed her tiny, dirty body, revolved it through chaos and squalor; ate entire slabs of Zetti chocolate or cooked a whole pan of oats with cocoa. She would consume the porridge all by herself; I never managed to get down anything that she offered me. In the afternoon her brothers and sisters would come home from school and work.

– Haven't had a fuck today, one older brother said to the other older brother, who then said:

– Do it with Katka's new friend, then.

I would run out of Katka's flat. Only to return. Every day after school, I was drawn to her place. I no longer held my breath, rummaged happily through the filthy clothes, ate porridge with cocoa as a mark of friendship. I told my parents that the school day had been extended and that this was the reason I was coming home late. My parents believed it for two whole months, then my mother caught me walking arm in arm with Katka. We'd stolen pink and white peppermint sticks – sweet, cheap fondant of the sort I was never allowed at home because it was common. In Katka's company I stuffed myself with big sticks of this delicacy, smearing my face and school dress with it.

My mother no longer allowed me to see Katka Lorenz. She picked me up from school every day and kept an eye out for Katka to make sure she wasn't anywhere near our villa. I got worse at school. In danger of having to retake the year, according to Fräulein Brinkmann.

Father hauled me off to a psychologist.

– Childish disobedience, apart from that she's normal. An intelligent child.

– What's the matter with you, Ehlchen?

Father drank cognac, and when Napoléon was conquered he attacked the Wacholder gin or the Polish vodka. Mother swept up dirt and glass shards from the parquet. She soon forgot all about the question of what

29

was wrong with me, my shame was *on the inside* after all – on the outside I was the doctor's little daughter with the big 'I' in the register.

Then came the parties. Our villa, a unique building within the industrial city of Leibnitz, was surely destined for them – and what with Father being the most eminent vascular surgeon, he had, after all, social duties to perform. The drunken, merry surgical team suggested to him: Throw a party, Doktor von Haßlau! It was a way out of the deathly silence, the state of meaninglessness, that Father fell into every night when he came back from the clinic. A condition that settled over him like a fog. Mother would open the door for him and the first fog would overwhelm him. Father would go into the kitchen and have a cognac or two, Mother would try to bat away the fog with sentences like: How was it at the clinic today? Or: There's roulade for dinner, just the way you like it, Ernst.

When I came home from school Father would be in his chair, while the corners of Mother's mouth would be twitching.

– He never wants to eat, she would say.

I'd eat two roulades for Father, even though I'd already be feeling sick from the fondant or sherbet that Katka brought to school and slipped to me under the exercise books.

It was when the parties started that I began to bunk off school with Katka.

– When you end up doing laundry, Katka said, you'll make more money than if you study at university anyway.

I'd remember this insight every time we made it back to school for the last lesson of the day and Mother would pick me up as if nothing had happened. We kept Fräulein Brinkmann off our backs with excuses, and threatened to shoot sharp staples at her if she squealed on us. At break time I would escape from her well-meaning grasp. It won me respect from the class.

It was Mother who insisted on the *parties*. She had no other desire than to rescue her spouse from his fog and to see him happy and distinguished again. *She* was somebody too, after all, and it had started so well in 1946, when she gave up her job as a radiographer for *him*, for him and the villa and this life. Mother organized the party and wrote invitations to Father's colleagues and our relatives. Father tore up the second lot of cards.

– No family, you know what they're like.

Uncle Schorsch's death came up in conversation. Father called Uncle Schorsch a fool, even though he hated the Russians too; they were the reason for his sadness, his fog… I was sent out of the room.

– Go and play in the garden, Ehlchen, there's going to be a party tonight.

Skipping school for the first couple of lessons was the best. Katka and I preferred it. We had discovered our new adventure: the canal. It flowed red, blue, grey or ochre through the city, swallowed the effluents from breweries, textile companies and machine manufacturers, and the outflow from the wool-dyeing factory. There was a smell of hops and malt hovering over it and at the bottom slimy plaits of grey algae drifted by. Katka knew a place under the Green Bridge for forbidden things and other thrills. Goldenrod and something that looked like giant rhubarb grew on the embankment. On the left bank, on the upwards slope, stood a little summer house, so dilapidated and overgrown by moss that we could have knocked it down with a few blows of our sticks.

– A nutcase lives there, said Katka.

In fact, as we waded into our adventure, the curtains of the little moss house twitched. I was frightened, but being with Katka spurred me on. Katka danced and stripped naked on the edge of the bank. She told me to do the same. I was embarrassed and worried that the filth in the canal would irritate my skin, but Katka told me about the elves who became more and more beautiful the longer they danced. Katka needed it of course, she danced and sang, and the swells of her body rose and sank in rhythm with *Let's twist agaiiin* and *Rock rock rock 'n' roll*. We would leap around naked on the banks of the canal whenever it was warm, laughing and fooling about. We put sprigs of goldenrod in our hair, ate the sour shoots of the canal rhubarb, got the runs, would shit ourselves empty, and screech whenever anyone looked down at us from the bridge. Eventually the police found out. One morning, two officers were standing at the railings of the Green Bridge. We spotted them straight away, turned off before the bridge and crossed to the other side of the street.

– Stop! the policemen shouted. Stay where you are!

We set off running, our satchels bouncing up and down on our backs, sandwiches and notebooks being thrown about inside. We knew it was all over, our adventure betrayed; and I knew there would be a terrible punishment, a terribly painful punishment, because the red 'I' in the register was my mark, while Katka had only a harmless thin pencil 'L' and didn't need to fear any repercussions. We raced down the street, the VoPo officers on our tails. We heard them panting and Katka, while still running, said we should double back. So we slowed down suddenly, turned on our heels and split up, heading back in the direction of the canal, up the grassy slope. I was overwhelmed by an excruciating stitch. Katka was too fat to keep going.

It was then that the door of the moss house opened and we were beckoned inside. I throbbed with fear right to the tips of my braids. Even my brave Katka bit her lip.

– Come in, said the witch.

I felt cold, hot, cold. I knew this voice, and the scent of resin. Frau Popiol lived here. The wig lit our way.

– We better get out of here, Katka whispered.

– No.

– The old bag's crazy, she'll eat us.

33

– She's my violin teacher.

– *You* can play the violin?

– Yes, Katka.

Frau Popiol led us inside: a room with a low ceiling, stuffed with piles of books, a single armchair, a pale-leaved rubber plant under the window. Beside the window a piano and next to it a set of shelves with countless records and tapes.

– I'll play something for you.

We stood in silence, two first-year pupils, I in my blue and white crocheted dress, Katka in a shabby skirt that belonged to her older sister. Frau Popiol picked a record from her collection.

I was afraid once more, I could already hear all the violin virtuosos in the whole world, could already hear Frau Popiol's sharp voice: ungifted, hopeless. Oh yes, Frau Popiol had seen us dancing the twist, dancing to rock 'n' roll – vulgar, disreputable music that was banned at our school, in dance halls and everywhere.

– Please, we won't ever do it again, I said.

And there it was once more. This small gesture of happiness. Frau Popiol's fingers stroked my hair, and she laughed deeply and mockingly.

– I've got something better than 'the twist'.

Inside the little moss house we listened to serious, urgent music which was far too grown up for us.

– You're an intelligent child, Frau Popiol said over the music, while Katka, mesmerized, swayed her body.

34

– Come again if you like.

– Yes, I said. Can Katka come too?

Frau Popiol nodded. She opened the kitchen door. Kurt had been standing behind it, eavesdropping. He was now allowed to enter the room. He waddled in on his duck feet, grinning. Then he stood in front of Katka. His head was shaking. As he danced awkwardly and off the beat, Katka mimicked his movements.

– Is the kid sick?

– No, Frau Popiol said. He can *really* dance.

When Frau Popiol finally sent us back to school, it was almost midday. I caught sight of Father's company car in front of the building. Fräulein Brinkmann had called Father, she had dared to snitch on us. Father got out of the car in his white coat. Children gathered around him. Look how tall he is! What a moustache! A doctor! A real doctor!

Father didn't scold me. Instead he sat in on our class, *observing*. The little chicken tried her best during the lesson. My classmates behaved impeccably, out of respect for our guest. Father sat right at the back in the corner on a tiny school chair. White and handsome, he gave off the mysterious scent of the hospital. Fräulein Brinkmann was nervous. Her weak voice petered out into a croak. She had summoned Father to chastise me. She'd ordered *punishment*, righteousness.

Father:

– My daughter doesn't play truant.

Fräulein Brinkmann:

– Unfortunately she does. She keeps bad company. But I as her teacher can't forbid her from going around with Katka Lorenz.

In the middle of the maths class, my father rose to his feet.

Fräulein Brinkmann flinched.

– Maybe Herr Doktor von Haßlau would like to tell us how he makes people better.

– No. Then, in a more friendly tone, towards the class: Another time perhaps.

Father employed someone to help out around the house. He went ahead with it in an act of defiance against the state.

– *State*, he said at the dinner table, a word that I should take note of.

– Repeat after me: *state*, the state's against us having help at home.

I didn't understand why anyone would mind my mother receiving help, or not want the dirt in the villa's countless rooms to be finally conquered. The help was called Frau Schramm. Mother gave her the kneeling cushion with the wax cloth and told her what to do. Then she had time for me. She took me to school every morning and picked me up every afternoon. The other children made fun of me. *Mollycoddled*, they called me. Katka was only mine now at break time. Beneath the horse chestnut in the schoolyard we made plans of escape and adventures, but we were being watched: zealous teachers on break-time duty or, even worse, older children. They stood behind us, next to us, and kept us apart:

– Katka Lorenz, take away the wastepaper bins immediately, and Gabriela von Haßlau has blackboard duty.

Sullenly I wiped the board in silence and waited for my mother. But Katka returned fire: staples, apple cores. She built plastic stink bombs, tore up the register.

– She'll end up in a home, I heard someone say.

Mother helped me with my homework while old Frau Schramm dusted, polished and waxed our villa. I made progress and found learning to write almost enjoyable. Father came home from work later every day. He thundered through the kitchen: he wanted to start a private practice, the *state* wouldn't allow it, but *he*, Ernst von Haßlau, would make it happen. That word *state* again, which belonged to Father, which came from deep within his broad chest soaked in cognac and which left barely any space for *me*. Mother told Father about my improving performance at school.

– We haven't taken enough care of her, Ernst, but everything's fine now.

– Everything's fine now, babbled Father. He poured out a large Napoléon, clamped his hand around the glass, raised it, inhaled, drank.

– Ernst!

– From now on we're going to throw parties, Christiane. We're somebodies!

Two semicircular sheets of paper made from the bags I found in the park, now filled with writing. I sense a future within me: something could come of my story, a success that could take me from this point to a better place – out from under the bridge, maybe into a little room of my own, maybe something even better. But what does that mean, better? I can't imagine it, and if I were to write about a better world, I would be doing so as a stranger to it.

It's the end of the working day for the few businesses in Leibnitz that are still going. Cars surge across my bridge, the canal slowly returns to its natural colour: a grey brown. I'm clocking off too. Raise myself up. I have to admit that sitting to write under a bridge isn't the most comfortable thing, but what can I do? It's cool and shady down here and no one pays any attention to me. There'll be supper at the shelter. A useful institution; they don't let you fall into the last hole, you get food, clothing, a chance to wash. You're still a somebody. But most people don't know who they are. Boozing and dossing – what a life! *They* don't know how to tell their story. They've just fallen. Right to the bottom. I'm not one of them.

Dusk. Feels good to have worked. I'll go and eat at the shelter, brush my teeth, then maybe a trip to the cinema.

There's always enough money for food and the cinema. The welfare office doesn't forget us. Not completely. Not so you fall into the last hole. *Not on our watch*. Fellini's playing at the Bali. The Capitol and Babylon are closed. The Bali then. *La Strada*. It's nice sitting in a comfy cinema seat. An old film: the poor girl who goes mad because of her existence and because of her love. And that bastard, that Zampanò, a lonely drunkard. My eyes close. I wake up with a broom thumping against my legs.

– Get out, you stupid Binka! Sleeping in the cinema, what's that about?

The broom sweeps me outside. I stagger into the summer night, my bag of things under my arm. The streets of Leibnitz are dead. The Three Roses is the only place where anyone's still up having a beer. The man in the cinema called me a Binka. How did he know? I shouldn't let myself go like this, dossing like that, like I'd been stacking boxes of apples in the market all day. I can't go back to sleep straight away. You have to be *dead tired* to be able to sleep under a bridge. If you're only drowsy you start to shiver and get scared of the canal and the darkness. It's only eleven o'clock and I'm wide awake and can't sleep. Where is there for me to go in Leibnitz? The shelter has places to sleep. Maybe... I won't go to the shelter. I walk into the Three Roses.

The bar: tiny, not even twenty square metres, two high tables to stand at, the wooden bar covered with stickers for Berlin FC, Olympia 2000, Test the West. Behind the

bar: Semmelweis-Märrie, weighing 300 kilos, serves
Pilsner beer and clear schnapps half a centimetre under
the measure line. I order a cola, then boldly join the
men, Rampen-Paul and Atze, Klunker-Lupo and Noppe,
the owners of the Green Bridge and the Sunday Bridge.
There's a woman among them too: *Angschelick*, she slob-
bers. A test of courage. The cola: sweet, brown, warm.

    – Wouldn't you rather a beer?

The Three Roses grin with the stumps of their teeth.

    – No. Don't smoke either.

    – Who are you, then?

    – Gabriela von Haßlau.

The Three Roses laugh, shriek, stamp their feet with
joy. You don't get a laugh like that every day, nearly fell
off my stool – *von* Haßlau! Stand firm. Just cola. But
that doesn't make you tired either. An apricot brandy
as well? Fine by me. The night will be twice as sweet.

    – Where do you live, Gabrüüüella *fffon* Haßlau?

Skinny, balding Noppe, who's doing the asking, and
who always gives the guys a laugh, drops a curtsy.

    – The Wet Fart Hotel, I say. The Three Roses are in
stitches. Lupo, tattooed up to the bridge of his nose,
sways over to me from the neighbouring table:

    – Know anyone?

    – Nope.

Klunker-Lupo has a hole in his forehead the size of
a cherry. He sticks a lit cigarette stump in it. I bang on
the table.

– Not yet I don't!

The peace treaty is sealed. Another apricot brandy to get me tired. Glues your soul together. Things must be going well, Gabriela, for you to end up here. Brandy. Cola. Just to get me tired so I'm feeling fresh for work in the morning… Rampen-Paul puts his right arm around my shoulder, pushes his man boobs up against me, leads my hand holding the little schnapps glass – where? The glass falls, tinkles, apricot brandy soaks into the muck on the floor. I feel the corduroy of Rampen-Paul's trousers stiff with filth and beer. Paul presses my fingers against his fly. A filthy snigger from Atze, who's offering himself up too.

– Get off!

I tread into the brandy, grab my bag of things – out!

The Three Roses is now behind me. Leibnitz is sleeping. The Green Bridge and the Sunday Bridge are occupied. The first night under *my* bridge. So tired I'm ready to drop. Lay out the corrugated cardboard, then a towel, then my body, then the new blanket from the shelter. Close my eyes, lying in the open green of nature, a little brook flows by, not malty and full of hops, but a clear forest stream, rats, deer, a little moss house, stalactites as long as sugar loafs, are you by any chance called Binka? Or Ehlchen? Too tired to say. Whoever knows falls down the last hole.

I wake in the morning, face and blanket wet from the dripstone water. The slopes of the embankment are fresh and green, goldenrod is in bloom, wild field poppies, dandelions. I'm shivering and even though I slept straight through I have a headache. I consider what to do so I don't get drenched again. Sleeping *next* to the bridge is as good as not having a place to sleep at all. Look for lodging at the shelter? They'd throw me out and send me to the welfare office – or hell. Who knows? They don't begrudge you a breakfast, but nothing more. Crap institution. I take coffee and rusks from the shelter anyway, stick rolls and sausages up my shirt for worse times and steal a roll of grey loo paper. That'll help me continue my story. A once-in-a-century summer! And my second day as a freelance author begins.

– We're somebodies!

Party was the new word.

– Repeat after me, Ehlchen: par-ty! It's American.

Father stroked his moustache. I sensed something forbidden behind this word, something similar to my deal-ings with Katka Lorenz. Father *just did it*, without fear of being caught, did what the *Russians* tried to *spoil* for you! He roared through the villa, frothing with indignity.

Mother wrote the invitations. I was given the task of drawing something on every card: a flower or a star.

– But no reds stars, Mother said, draw a yellow one or a blue one or a tree.

I licked the tips of the colouring pencils so the draw-ings would be vibrant. At our first party, one of Father's colleagues from the clinic brought me a real felt-tip pen.

– Who shall we invite?

– Esteemed colleagues and artists, decreed Father, no Party bigwigs, no assistant doctors, no nurses, no family.

I wasn't sure if *I* was included in this category and tried my best to make the stars and trees especially beautiful. I was excited to see who would come. I secretly hoped for Frau Popiol. In my eyes she was one of the artists. Leibnitz doesn't show off its artists, I heard Father say, but they're there!

Frau Popiol wasn't on the list. I was disappointed. The buffet stretched from the music room through to the living room. The double doors were taken off their hinges, the parquet was waxed. For three days Mother and Frau Schramm cooked, stirred, crafted delicacies. I was allowed to add paprika and parsley to the canapés, decorate the salad, line up the bottles of drink. I was happy. The strange shine of the villa banished my boredom. Something big was coming. On the day the buffet was fully laid out, Mother picked me up from school an hour early. I relished bunking off with permission. My parents were right: *we were somebodies*. We had power over Fräulein Brinkmann, who *had* to let me leave, we had power over all the school directors, all the assistant doctors and all the nurses in the whole world.

Father in his grey suit and black tie was tall and handsome, almost exotic with his black hair and waxed moustache. Mother wore a green silk dress, strings of pearls and high-heeled shoes. I wore a dirndl, white knee-high socks, red leather shoes, with my braided hair up.

And then there were the guests. There were senior doctors and actors, orchestra directors, soloists and painters. Twenty, thirty people wearing peculiar outfits and special perfumes that Mother called *festive*. They made their entrances and presented my parents with gifts; they brought me Sarotti chocolate or Mickey Mouse notebooks, delightfully forbidden things. Our villa filled with people. They laughed and mingled around, my father was somebody, he was mentioned often, and frequently referred to by his full name and title, Obermedizinalrat Ernst von Haßlau, and Father waved graciously each time.

Suddenly I was sent to bed. It's nine o'clock, that's when children *must* go to bed. Frau Schramm, who up until that point had been busy in the kitchen, was given the task of undressing and washing me and bundling me off to bed. I resisted, kicked out, wanted to stay, caused a scene, threw myself onto the parquet. Mother was mortified, Father reached for the Napoléon, the guests whispered in awkwardness. I knocked a bowl of dessert off the table. Then a young man grabbed me, lifted me up and carried me out of the room. He had me in an armlock, making me defenceless.

In the hallway, the man said that if I was a good girl he would show me something. I promised with a whimper. The man had shoulder-length curly blond hair. He was called Samuel and was an actor.

– Watch this, kid.

Samuel went into the bathroom and closed the door behind him. All of a sudden I heard a gruesome scream, groaning, and a shiver ran down my spine. I wanted to shout for help, but then the bathroom door opened and Samuel toppled onto the floorboards with a crash. A broomstick was sticking out from under his right armpit. He was dead. I screamed and wanted to run back to the music room, but the corpse rose from the dead.

– Did you like it?

I nodded, embarrassed. Then Samuel ran against the hallway door and I was sure that he must have broken all his ribs and cracked his skull. But he was still in one piece. He carried me into the kitchen. Frau Schramm was polishing glasses. Samuel snatched the cloth from her and got to work. He tossed glasses and plates, juggled frying pans, knives, forks. Frau Schramm and I were in awe. Samuel balanced the knife sharpener on his nose – it fell and landed on his foot. He hopped about holding his toes and I laughed so hard I cried. Frau Schramm kept watch at the kitchen door while Samuel showed us yet more incredible feats until my head felt like it was about to burst from laughing.

The next morning was Saturday. I was the only one who had to leave the house, as I had school. I clambered over the remains of the party. The villa was a wreck.

Frau Schramm was nowhere to be seen. I was still tired and picked at the leftover meat salad. Whole batteries of Napoléon and other empty bottles rolled across the parquet. I called for Father and Mother. I found Father in the bathroom sitting on the toilet – his suit trousers thrown off, his legs naked. He was leaning over the washbasin, sleeping. The basin was blocked with vomit. Father was breathing, so I knew he wasn't dead. I retched and went into the bedroom. I stood in the doorway. In my parents' bed lay my mother and the young, blond Samuel. Both naked. I looked at them for a long time. To tell the truth, it was a much more pleasant sight than that of my father, almost like a painting. Leaning against the glass-topped dressing table watching them sleeping, I had the urge to lie down with them. But I had to go to school. Every day I felt a more and more urgent need to be punctual and hard-working, to show what I had within me. So Mother had to be woken. I took the Flakon hairspray off the dresser, pressed the pump and sprayed the sticky haze onto my mother's stomach. Which woke Samuel. He jumped out of bed like a tomcat.

– Ohgodohgod, he whispered, taking my hand and leading me out of the bedroom.

– Someone's in the bathroom, I said.

Samuel guffawed. He *never* washed anyway.

I helped him to find his clothes strewn around the villa.

– Ohgodohgod!

He shook his blond thatch of hair, got dressed and said:

– Watch this!

He picked up an empty Napoléon, tipped it up and drank and drank all of the schnapps-scented air in the bottle. His body jerked, his eyes rolled, he swayed and fell onto the parquet like a marionette cut from its strings. I couldn't wake him. At first I laughed, then I tickled him. Blood ran out of his mouth – I was horrified, tore out of the room. Samuel found me and pulled a tomato skin out from between his teeth.

– Did you like it?

Samuel began to visit our family a lot. He played the Archangel Gabriel at the theatre. Father was proud of him, even though he only went to the theatre for *prestige*. The word *prestige* belonged to my father, but Samuel's body belonged to my mother. When Father was at the clinic and I was playing hopscotch in the garden, I sometimes saw Samuel through the gaps in the blinds. On those days Mother was especially kind and generous.

– You can play in the street today if you like, Ehlchen.

Samuel always left the house via the veranda stairs, and it was only when he was officially invited that he would step, gallant and debonair, out of the front door. Father would boast about their friendship and Mother would smile. Whenever he saw me he collapsed heart-stricken to the floor or rammed into a wall. I was always shocked, as if for the very first time.

The parties became more frequent. Guests would fill our villa every fortnight. A written invitation was soon no longer necessary to visit the doctor. Assistant doctors, nurses and other people without *prestige* didn't dare show up anyway. Leibnitz worshipped us, and gossiped about us too. My parents lost track of the guests. Every party brought someone new and guests would bring others with them: an artist from Berlin, a writer from Dresden, a circus director, even a neurologist from Hamburg. Men entered and introduced themselves as *someone*, nice men from the fields of art and medicine, they ate and drank and talked. They talked with me too – a Dr Schneider or Professor Müller or Herr Labuhn or whatever they were called. All of them led wild, urgent conversations. Late in the evenings, when I would be trying to go to sleep, I heard the word *state* and the word *nonetheless*, and wild dreams followed me well into the next day. The parties of Obermedizinalrat von Haßlau were the talk of the town.

A voice called me from the garden. The party was in full swing. I snuck out of the house thinking a guest couldn't find the entrance. Katka was waiting for me in the garden, wrapped in a dark coat.

– You going to let me in?

– Are you crazy? It's already late, your mother will…

– I ran away.

– For goodness' sake, Katka.

– You letting me in or what?

I smuggled Katka in through the veranda. We hid in the playroom. Katka gawped.

– Look at all the stuff you've got.

– There's loads more, I added.

I fetched pâté and a bottle of beer for Katka. We giggled, drank beer and played dressing up. I fetched my mother's wedding dress from her wardrobe and put it on.

– Oh, my princess, bowed Katka, lifting the seam of her grubby knitted dress.

I demanded nasally:

– Katka, the smelling salts! I'm going to faint!

Katka brought me the bottle of beer and I took a deep swig.

– Come on, come on, now clean my shoes!

Katka spat on my slippers. Then she lost interest. I continued to boss her around.

– Comb my hair!

Katka didn't want to listen. I pushed her against the wall.

– I let you in.

We were intoxicated from the beer and my mother's wedding dress. Katka wanted to be the princess. I wouldn't allow it. Don't know what it was that made me treat her so harshly – a cool rage, disgust at Katka's insignificance, or the secret longing to run away. Like Katka. Katka left the villa before midnight. I had no idea where she slept that night. We met again at school the next day. Fräulein Brinkmann wanted to know if we'd been crying. Our faces were red, puffy, like we'd gone a couple of rounds in a fight.

Day in, day out: dripstone shelter apricot brandy writing sleeping dripstone… I reject whatever the welfare office offers me: work in a launderette or delivering the post. I can't, won't. My story captivates me. I wake up one night; I jolt out of a dream, the shock breaks the illusion: where am I? I scream, shaking, the unimaginable: underneath a bridge. Under a blanket, on cardboard, like a tramp. Total, utter scum. I'm dreaming, I've lost my mind – ha! Neither. I reel, bang my forehead against the slick stone of the bridge vault; I've known this canal since my childhood – it stinks of malt and slurry. I gather my things together, I climb up the canal bank trembling with fear and dismay. The moss house – now just a ruin. I leave it behind and run through the Leibnitz night. Home! Where? Wherever you want, says a voice. I've gone mad. They're after me, searching for me. How long have I been sleeping under a bridge? Where did this scratchy grey blanket come from? Where did this cardboard, these bags, this toilet paper come from? I'm sick, insane – in this moment I see it clearly.

The policeman asks me for my identification card and place of residence.

– I went out into the wide world to learn fear.

– You'll learn about it very soon, says the policeman.

Takes me down the cop shop. It's bright and warm there, the officers on duty smoke and type on their old typewriters. They're tired, while I've never been so awake.

– Blimey! a peanut-shaped face snaps at me. Name, address, offence.

– Offence? My name is Gabriela von Haßlau.

The peanut makes a call.

– A *fffon* Haßlau. Yeah, *fffon*, that's what she said! the policeman yaps into the mouthpiece.

I find myself in the admissions of the psychiatric department of the state hospital. Here again, I think. I hear words like *bag lady* and *cuckoo*.

– NO! I say. I don't want any of this. I'm a writer.

Every answer is a mistake. They lock me in the dormitory, where I can finally get some rest among raving lunatics, exhausted after hours of questioning. The next day I'm free again. They couldn't find anything pathologically wrong with me. Find myself back on the streets where I've been living for weeks, remember my mission. Writing, just writing. The summer is warm, almost motionless. There's only one place that I live. I steal a poster from an advertising pillar. On the front it says: 'David Dreamer, greatest magician of all time'. The back is white, empty, good enough to continue my story.

My husband has lost his *prestige*, I heard Mother tell Frau Schramm while she helped her slice beans in the kitchen. I guessed that it meant a lot to Father, and I secretly began searching for his prestige at home and in the street. If only I knew what *prestige* looked like. I felt no particular love for my father; instead I observed him, like I would a wild animal. Sometimes I was allowed to sit on his lap and smell the clouds of Napoléon, other times I would get a slap for no reason, mostly when the Napoléon was empty or if he and my mother had had another argument about the word *state*. I asked Mother about Father's *prestige*, where I could find it. Mother smiled sadly and said:

– She who eavesdrops gets big ears.

Frau Schramm simply sighed and pointed to the empty bottles of schnapps in the bin.

– It's none of my business, but Herr Doktor…

I'd just come in from the garden when I heard a crash in the villa. Father must have fallen down the stairs drunk. I rushed into the house. It wasn't Father but Samuel. The blond angel lay in the hallway without his shirt and trousers, both of his legs bloody. Mother came out of the bedroom pleading, wrapped in a bed sheet. Father stood before Samuel in his doctor's coat, pulled his stethoscope out of his bag and started whipping him. Samuel whimpered and the rubber tubing hissed. Father made the stethoscope swish, swish, swish. I threw myself between them.

– What do you all want from me! Father howled.

Samuel pulled himself up. He'd been caught this time and I wondered why he didn't seem ashamed.

Samuel hobbled out of the villa, but not without blowing Mother a mischievous kiss. Exhausted after this scene, Father fell asleep in his armchair. He'd been sent home early from the clinic. *Prestige*, I thought to myself, and began to fear my father.

My parents' divorce took place in the summer. I was thirteen years old and it seemed to me that I hadn't been present in the world until this day. I crawled underneath the veranda stairs looking for anything, found spiders and earthworms. Only semi-conscious, I walked up the stairs to the attic. It was hot with the batten doors closed. Beams, boxes and junk gave off a strong smell of wood. A thumb's width of dust had settled on the floor. It reeked of marten muck. Threads from old grey spider's webs hung from the wooden beams. In the webs, as if caught in a snare, were the white husks of skinned cross spiders. I rummaged around in the clutter, broke open boxes, ransacked baskets. I tried to cry. My parents' divorce was being played out downstairs in the music room. I sat on a heap of rags and waited among the creaking of the summer-heavy woodwork for tears. Next to me, in a trunk eaten by woodworm, I found books. I lined up everything this trunk offered: eight volumes of *Goldköpfchen*, six volumes of *Nesthäkchen*, a number of hiking and nature stories – my grandmother's books. I opened the first one, began to spell my way through the old typeface, and soon I had grown accustomed to it. The whole day and half the night I read stories. I was now grateful that the tears had failed to come, that a world had opened up to me. I read book after book. When school was over for the day I would climb up into the attic. At school I remained an average, introverted student, withdrawn, insignificant. Father had forbidden me to join the Young Pioneers. Farce! He babbled something about the church and went straight to the school director. Only Katka Lorenz with her boundless enthusiasm succeeded in motivating me every now and again to do something wild. That's how she persuaded me to turn up at the flag ceremony wearing an enormous Pioneer scarf. She got hold of a blue sheet about the size of a tablecloth and wrapped it around my neck and shoulders. The ends hung to the ground and the knot was the size of a head of kohlrabi!

– Just stand in the first row.

She promised me a surprise if I dared to do it. I accepted the dare. It was the final ceremony the Pioneers had to attend before they were old enough to become members of the Free German Youth. So, having never had to attend any ceremonies before, I stood in the front row. The giant blue cloth glowed and the semicircle of students spluttered with suppressed laughter. Then the director spotted me. He stopped speaking halfway through his address, stepped towards me – I held my breath – he walked passed me, waded through the rows, grabbed Fräulein Brinkmann, dragged the chicken to the front, into the middle of the semicircle. She got what I deserved.

The same evening she came to see my father in tears. His roaring laughter must have been the final straw. Fräulein Brinkmann was off sick for two weeks. As a reward for the successful prank, Katka Lorenz took me into the bathroom with her.

– I'll show you something.

A pair of dark-red blots in the toilet bowl. They belonged to Katka. And they frightened me. Katka's time had come.

Mother moved in with Samuel. When she said goodbye, she kissed me and said with feigned cheerfulness:

– You can visit us anytime you want, Dresdner Straße 8 – you hear, Dresdner 8, fourth floor!

She squeezed my hand, Samuel did his usual 'Murder victim staggers out of the bathroom' number – then I was standing there alone. In the days and weeks that followed I kept mostly to the kitchen with Frau Schramm. Father had night duty more often than before, but would come home early from the clinic more often too. All parties were cancelled. Father barely spoke any more. He sat in his chair and slept, or drank Napoléon. He hardly ate anything any more. And one Sunday when I came across him in the bathroom he had white hair.

– Do you see, Ehlchen, he said very quietly, *this* is what I've earned.

His moustache had stayed dark. I gave him some awkward compliments.

– It doesn't look awful.

– Fucking *state*! Father cursed.

He threw a vase against the glass cabinet in the living room. Both shattered. He hammered wildly on the piano, shredded the bedclothes and curtains in a senseless rage. He wasn't chief medical officer any more. Without the practical Frau Schramm, Father would have fallen apart in no time at all. As Father got into the worst scraps with Napoléon and Consorts, as he lay helplessly paralysed on the floor and an ambulance had to be called, as he was banned from working and offered rehab, as I wanted to move in with Samuel, as Frau Popiol crossed my path, here, there, in distressing dreams, as I—

– Your father has to have a long rest in hospital. A shock from the booze like that takes a while to get over. He has to get it all out of his system. But, Ehlchen, when he comes back, all that stuff will be gone!

Frau Schramm destroyed Father's stash of alcohol and swore to watch him like a hawk from now on.

– Not a drop more, nope. The Herr Doktor...

Father returned from the hospital and swallowed whatever he could find: aftershave and Klarofix window cleaner, eau de cologne, hair tonic, Fagusan cough drops. He drank the rum food essence, begged Frau Schramm for a glass of beer or a teeny little glass of Napoléon. Just a tiny one. Frau Schramm stood firm and locked all the doors and windows so Father couldn't escape. He was signed off sick. I found Frau Schramm's behaviour cruel. Still, I was grateful to her. Every day Father's shakes got worse.

– Cold turkey! Frau Schramm diagnosed.

Father grew softer and more and more helpless. He sat in his chair for hours on end, listening to the radio. He would reach out to me sometimes – his hands cold and fluttering, as if he wanted to say something. He drank a lot of coffee, feasted on bags of sweets. Once he said:

– I'm going to leave this place.

He stayed. Over time he became fat, two of his incisors fell out. That's how I saw him every day. It was as if I had nothing to do with him, and he didn't mind. I skulked around as if only half alive. I enjoyed school less and less, the word *state* came up in lessons more and more, I was tired for no apparent reason. It was worst in civic education. Once I even fell asleep. Herr Wanzke, our teacher for civics and geography, sent bits of chalk and board rubbers flying from his desk, lecturing all the while:

– The sovereignty of the working people, internalized within the foundation of democratic centralism, is the basic principle of state-building.

Wanzke snitched on me to the director. The director: I was a special case, I couldn't be easily classified. But careful, colleague! – referencing the red 'I' in the register. Fräulein Brinkmann was form tutor of a first-year class again. Ours, class 8c, had shed their Pioneer scarves and had received new blue Free German Youth shirts. Once again, I wasn't allowed to join. Father was against it.

Time: a board rubber plump with water. Father said he was dry. Only the books in the attic made me feel better. I didn't know any other way to pass the time. Visits to my mother and Samuel became more and more boring. They only talked about theatre, and my mother had lately started talking about clothes and hairstyles. She slipped me money: buy something pretty. Samuel ran against the wall and I laughed without laughing. I tried to become close with Katka again, but Katka didn't want to shoplift in the cooperative any more, or revel in our childish canal dancing. Since showing me her period blood she had become dedicated to art. Katka was constantly doodling during lessons: mad geometric figures, wild things, grotesque faces – she painted over everything, crossed out, erased.

– Art, she said proudly.

Break time. The classroom emptied. Katka stuck two dozen of her artworks on the classroom walls. When Wanzke saw this he shouted:

– Volunteers!

No one knew what he meant, no one stood up from their desk.

– Grumert, Dreyer, Haßlau – to the front!

We obeyed. Wanzke dunked the board rubber in water and put it in Grumert's hand.

– Throw it! Whoever hits the most pictures in Katka's gallery gets a One in civics.

Grumert threw, the wet rubber clattered against the wall. No one laughed. Wanzke repeated the process, plunged the rubber in water. Petra Dreyer let it fall to the floor.

– I won't do it.

– Five! Wanzke's voice snapped. He soaked the rubber for a third time.

– You could use a One, Fräulein von Haßlau, Wanzke said, grinning.

Then I threw the rubber and hit one first time. It sprayed out from all sides, colour streamed over the walls – fetch the rubber, back to the front, aim and – splat! Another one of Katka's dumb pictures. Still no laughter from the class. I kept throwing. The room was dripping from the slaughter, even Wanzke was uneasy about it: how was he ever going to get the walls clean again? When all the pictures were sodden and had fallen to the floor, I left the room. I felt sick and hung my head over the sink in the toilets. Nothing came out. So I washed and scrubbed myself, saw a stupid face in the mirror and all I could think was: You get your black hair from your father. I began to cry. The floodgates opened and I wailed, shaking from convulsions, disorientated, helpless.

– Give it a rest, someone said. Katka. She gave me a huge man's handkerchief.

– It's not that clean.

I blew my nose and immediately started wailing again. Katka explained that it was still art, even if the pictures were now wet and torn. I fell into Katka's arms, she patted me on my back. I'd wailed myself wide awake. Awakened. Katka Lorenz and I went back into the classroom hand in hand. Wanzke didn't say a word when I crossed out the One in the register.

My sickness is called *awakening*. Every time I stop writing it threatens to clear my head. It's the only thing I'm afraid of. In September the once-in-a-century summer draws to a close. I'm starting to freeze at night. The goldenrod withered long ago and the canal rhubarb's gone brown and limp. The regulars from the Green Bridge and the Sunday Bridge close ranks. They decide when it's time for bed in the Three Roses. The end of the day recedes further and further. I go along with it: cola and apricot brandy. I don't like following what the old soaks are talking about. I keep shtum in their warm midst. They keep telling the same stories, prison anecdotes, their women troubles. They insult me so often it's unbearable. I only put up with it because I've got no other option. There are times when one of them doesn't show up. We raise a glass in his honour. Semmelweis-Märrie makes another sale.

– They want to close the dyeing factory.

A toast, a toast, a toast to the good times! The Three Roses is full to the brim. I'm worried about my bridge. I'm plagued by the thought that someone new might take my spot. I leave the bar before everyone else and reclaim what's mine.

In the autumn there's free fruit from people's gardens and an extra blanket from the shelter. One of the cooks in the kitchen gives me a tip about a barn I could sleep in.

– In *Mecklenburg*, have a look there. *You* don't have to be sleeping under no bridge, *Frol*lein.

– I know Mecklenburg. I've still got a long way to go before I'm in the last hole!

The cook taps her temple.

– Daft.

I shower every day. I keep myself clean, unlike the customers of the Three Roses. I've even learned that the last shower has to be ice cold. Then you freeze a bit less. I usually sleep well with two blankets. It's only when it rains and the canal rises that I get cold. The canal can overflow. It's not even two metres wide and cradled in a concrete bed. When this happens, I spend my nights on the slope of the bank, buried in a narrow cavity between the bridgehead and the street. Strong rain does have the advantage of cleaning the canal. The stronger flow rakes up the dormant rubbish and the slurry-algae, the canal swirls fat and dark brown through Leibnitz. Even days after the rain the water is almost clear at times. And because the water hasn't changed colour for seven days, I now know for sure: the wool-dyeing factory has shut for good.

Wrapped up on a bench in Schiller Park, I shift back in time to my beginnings. I scavenge serviettes from a food stand, a couple of pages of paper only printed on one side from a skip. I write on them to hold off awakening.

Black spiders had nested under the cellar stairs again. This was where Katka showed me her art. She explained the wild scribbles, taught me to see colours, lines, shade, light. Katka confessed to me that she had kissed a man.

– Who?

– Wanzke. Down by the canal. To say sorry.

– And?

– And nothing. It's not a big deal.

Time and again I was repulsed by Katka. I couldn't make sense of her. She didn't look down on Wanzke the way I did. She was a member of the Free German Youth and said all sorts of things I couldn't understand against the word *state*. I only surmised that she must have been against it because Wanzke kept her back after every civics class. I didn't understand what was up with her, but I was drawn to her anyway: grubby, fat, cheerful and carefree.

Father went back to work at the clinic and operated on varicose veins. He had new teeth made and dyed his hair black. He didn't touch another drop of Napoléon. Frau Schramm chalked it up as her success and keenly busied herself as a stirrer of milky drinks and tea. Father straightened himself out. He tried to be strict, to reign over the villa like he used to. He suddenly became interested in my schoolwork and paid attention to the company I kept. He didn't allow Katka Lorenz anywhere in the vicinity of the villa.

– She's a born loser.

I was supposed to go to extended secondary school after the eighth grade and then university. Wanzke explained to my father that this wouldn't be possible for a non-member of the Free German Youth. Social organization was a prerequisite to study at a socialist university. Father shouted at Wanzke in the middle of the school. He wielded a strange power over him. Wanzke cowered, small and wiry as he was, before Father's words about fairness and equality. I was on a flat Five in civics. At risk of having to retake the year. Father raged. His wrath was for the *system*, for the school, for my teacher Wanzke. If I had to retake a year, studying would be out of the question. Father's violent temper, his behaviour at home and his endless school visits infuriated me. It wasn't about me, it was about him. About his lost *prestige*. He wanted it back.

– Get your head down! he ordered. You're going to learn all this history rubbish and stay on the right side of that rat Wanzke. The time will come when these big shots will be in for it, Ehlchen, and then you'll see who we are.

– Who are we, then?

Father hit me. He'd never properly hit me before, but this question made him do it. From that day onwards I had no idea what I was doing. It all started when I put my hand up in the middle of civics, stood up and announced:

– Herr Wanzke, I know that you've been kissing a student.

Jeering laughter, from Katka too. The spindly Wanzke ducked down, fumbled with the register, wrote something in it. At break time he showed me a big red One in the space by my name.

– Do we understand one another, Gabriela?

The rumour of the kiss soon got legs at school, more Ones followed. I decided to join the Free German Youth. At dinner, Frau Schramm's knife fell from her hand and Father instantly left the table: I'd shown up wearing a blue shirt, with a written commendation in my schoolbag.

– Have you gone mad? Frau Schramm plucked at the blue material as if to check it was real. Father ranted that I was a stupid Binka! I'd sufficiently punished Father and had enjoyed defeating Wanzke. Everyone was astonished by my behaviour. The director summoned me to his office and congratulated me on my new standing in the class.

– Top notch, Gabriela Haßlau.

– *Von* Haßlau.

I knew what I was saying, and also didn't know, or I knew that I didn't know, and said anyway:

– Von, *fffon* Haßlau.

The director changed the subject: he'd heard that I might know... well, he meant I might be able to say whether Herr Wanzke...

– YES! I said clearly and loudly. YES.

My mouth spoke of its own accord. Yes, I knew. Civic education was postponed for the foreseeable future. A new teacher couldn't step in right away.

– You finished Wanzke, said Katka.

– Yes.

– He got time.

– Yes.

– Do you know *how* he kissed?

– Yes.

Katka left me standing there. I was suddenly alone. Wanted to get away. Where to? Wherever you want. I walked through the city. The city ended at the canal. The city always ended at the canal. Where to now? Yes or no. Wherever you want. I don't know where I want to go. Yes. No. I've never been kissed. Don't lie. On the canal there's a little house. Who lives in this little house? Yes or no. Steer clear of it. Why? Don't know, wherever you want. Dance by the canal. I can't dance. Completely unmusical. You don't know who you are. Yes. No. I walked and walked and couldn't go any further.

There was a poster on the advertising pillar in Leibnitz's Theatre Square:

ANTONIO VIVALDI

VIOLIN CONCERTO IN A MINOR, OP. 3

SOLOIST: MARIA ELKE POPIOL

It can't be. Madness. My teacher. My first kiss. I can play the violin. No, I can't. Ran home, changed my clothes, broke open my piggy bank.

– Where are you going?

– Wherever I want.

Back to Theatre Square. *The concert is about to begin.* I sat among a crowd of people, my body felt strange and meaningless. I feared that I was dreaming and Maria Elke Popiol wasn't *my* Frau Popiol. Then she came on and played. The red wig, backcombed into a heap, left me breathless. It was her. What music, sounds from an entire other *world*. She played effort-lessly well, witch, conjuror of fairy tales – *that* was music. Something unfamiliar to me.

– Play what I play, Gabriela!

And Frau Popiol played, the audience applauded, thunder, dachshund yapping, that's a vi-o-lin, music fades, where am I? Frau Popiol was famous, how could I have underestimated her, who is this woman? Vivaldi, Violin Concerto in A Minor, Opus 3! Her red hair blew all around, come with me! It was *my* violin playing that music. I buried my face in my hands – I never wanted to wake up again, never wanted to hear anything else. Why didn't I know who Frau Popiol was?

After the concert I lurched into the night. I wandered around the concert hall. Evening, the first time out on my own, I've ended up someplace or other. Frau Popiol and her son Kurt. I ran into her arms.

– Gabriela! cried Frau Popiol.

Kurt, appallingly grown, slapped his hands together.

– How did you like it? Frau Popiol stroked my hair, admired its blackness.

– Yes. I was horrified. How obediently this YES came out of my mouth, but this time I meant it. I wanted to walk Frau Popiol home, the famous violinist, who had let me experience my first happiness…

– Go home, Gabriela.

Frau Popiol gave me her hand. In the darkness her hair was black like mine. I wanted to tell Frau Popiol that only *she* could help me, that only *she* knew what was to become of me – and the kiss, she doesn't remember? – no, I've never kissed a boy, and the records, don't you remember?… I clung onto her arm. Kurt became distressed, angry. His supple, chubby hands struck against me. Frau Popiol freed herself from my grip.

– This has gone too far, Gabriela.

The nights are getting colder and my blankets are damp. My trousers and shirt have holes and yellowed spots.

Need to get a warm jumper from the clothes bank at the shelter, leather shoes. Preparations. For what? Leibnitz has almost completely shut down. Only the brewery and the old industrial plant are still in operation. You have to get to the Three Roses *before* six o'clock to find standing room. Semmelweis-Märrie has taken on Klunker-Lupo as a glass-washer.

– He's out of the woods, the others say, and Klunker-Lupo washes glasses like he's possessed. It's warm in the Three Roses. But Semmelweis-Märrie doesn't want to hear about 'staying open all night'.

– I'm not your mama.

The only way I can get to sleep is if I eat something just before bedding down. A half-empty stomach stops me from falling asleep, then I freeze, even with two blankets. The canal rhubarb has withered, it hangs in the water like brown guts until it's yanked out by the current. Good for making a fire, though. Next to the bridge, a really small one that doesn't bother the cops, that scares off the rats. Now and again I think it might be good to hang out with the others. But who are the others? Down-and-out illiterate tramps! *I'm* not destitute, just trying to prove myself. And anyway. The blanket up over both ears. The canal murmurs. Stars blink in the autumnal sky. The first snow falls at the beginning of December. It freezes overnight. Wake up, red and blue fingers and toes, the top half of the blanket frozen from my breath. Keep writing. Writing more, that will help. I find a little corner in the canteen at the shelter for a couple of hours. The chaos disturbs me. They're all gawping at me, jostling, joking. Everyone's bored and just about keeping down their beer-dulled rage. When the shelter's closed we loiter down by the food stalls. Press ourselves in under the narrow roofs, right up against each other to fight off the first snow, a beer for breakfast, a can, two cans, three. The other more wholesome customers crave chips and bratwurst, greasy things, along with beer and bad coffee. Every now and again they drop something: a charred bit of sausage or a half-cooked chip; then it's a game, a competition, us versus the pigeons that hobble around on crippled feet, witlessly nodding, picking at scraps, the fatty junk, and we, because it's warm here, keep on the good side of the kiosk owners and keep asking for beer and keep chatting through the shit times because it's fucking cold. The first snow is always colder than the last, that's what they say, the ones who've survived a year already and don't wash any more because it stops you from cooling down, the feared sudden death, it always comes when you're doing all right. That girl Angschelick has already shuffled off. We rub our fingers together, new people come, everyone calls themselves something or other. They call me Binka.

From Theatre Square I walk in the direction of Schiller Park. The shortest way home. All hair is black in the dark. Kurt is stupid. The sky is full of violins. This has gone too far, Gabriela. Repeat after me: too far. I walk faster. The park: black, full of strangeness. The first night just for me. I wasn't allowed to follow her, she was famous, Maria Elke Popiol, the blues and Vivaldi, the kiss and Father's voice: She's sick.

– Give me your red hair, I said loudly into the darkness. I sat down on a bench and noticed that I'd been crying the whole time, gently and warmly. I closed my eyes.

They come from behind. One drags me from the bench, the other wrestles my bag from me. Lying in the foliage, I feel my head being pressed between two bare legs. The legs clamp around my throat. I only see leaves and grey Silastik socks with sagging elastic. The one holding me like a vice gathers up my hair, roughly divides it into three strands, braids a thick, long plait. I can still see only leaves and socks, both men groan and growl like animals. Now the other one kneels in front of my face in the leaves, his trousers pulled down to his ankles. I see the rod, while the one pinning me down swings the plait, makes it swish, back and forth, up and down, like a horsewhip. I close my eyes: white leaves, everything is just white leaves. My skull grips the plait tightly, he whips it: *Faster! faster!* The white leaves burn, my head is tugged upwards: *Keep your eyes open!* I see everything doused in lightning flashes, then the leg vice releases me. I lie in a soft autumnal bed. The one with the Silastik socks turns me onto my back, rips my skirt at the seam, forces my thighs apart. *Mygoodgirlmydarlingmybeauty*, he whispers. Pain to the tip of my plait. Lightning. The man's body falls onto me. He's heavy and warm underneath his shirt. *Mygoodgirlmydarlingmybeauty*. He twitches limply. Come on! the other shouts. It's a stupid *Binka*! I lie there free for a handful of seconds. Then one of them grabs my arm and the other a knife. They cut a cross into my arm between my hand and elbow. One says: I didn't want that to happen. The other: Come on, will you! She's just a Binka!

I crawled through the damp leaves, my arm brown with blood and dirt. I crawled across the Leibnitz cobbles to the police station.

– I've been attacked.

– Sit down. Name! Address! Age! What are you doing on the street alone at night? Concert? Attacked? Where? When? Comrade Paffrath, take down the details. In the park? What's that, show me.

– They cut it into me.

– Who? When? Cut what? Are you mad?

– They called me Binka.

– Wait a minute, Comrade Paffrath. *What* did they say? Binka? Impossible. You're lying. You're making it up.

– They had a knife, that's how they cut me, and they said Binka!

– Give it a rest, girl. Are you telling us everything? What did the men do? One thing at a time, in the right order!

– They attacked me, two men, in the park, the knife, they said Binka and cut me.

– You're trying to slander the state. You're lying. You cut your own arm. We'll get to the bottom of this. Comrade Paffrath, write down: self-mutilation.

– They attacked me, two men. They said Binka!

– Where do you live? Father? What, a doctor? Ah, that fits.

I was taken to the clinic. The wound needed dressing.

– Clean incision, it will scar.

The doctor snipped the last stitch, dabbed the wound clean.

They came to see my father and said: Your daughter cut her own arm. *You* will have to suffer the consequences. Defamation of the state, Herr Doktor von Haßlau. They went to see Mother and Samuel and said: Your daughter cut her own arm. Self-mutilation. Mother didn't believe them, Samuel showed them the door. They went to see Samuel at the theatre and told him that his employment at the municipal playhouse was no longer required. They came to see Father and said: There's a scar, your daughter's showing it off, you will suffer the consequences! They came to see Frau Schramm in the kitchen and asked her if she was willing to work for this family any longer. They went to see Mother and asked whether she would rather see Samuel again or her daughter. They came to my school and asked Grumert-Thomas, Dreyer-Petra, Lorenz-Katka and all the others what kind of pupil I was, what my behaviour was like. They came to see Father and said: If you don't get rid of your daughter's scar you'll soon be replaced. They went to see Mother and said that they knew what happened to her brother Georg... They went to see Mother and couldn't find her at her apartment. They came to see Father and asked: Where is your ex-wife? They came to my school and escorted me home. And said: You shouldn't tell lies. You're lying! They came to see Father and Father took me to the clinic. None of his colleagues were willing to do it. Father transplanted a circular piece of skin from my upper thigh onto the place on my arm. After the operation they still came to Father, to school, to Frau Schramm. And they came to me and said:

– This won't be the last time we see each other.

– *You're* a Binka! squawks Klunker-Lupo from behind the bar. Everyone laughs, grinning toothlessly, frozen. I write crouched against the heater, sentence by sentence.

– *She* can write, roars old Fisherman-Kurt, plagued by a hacking cough, through the haze of the barroom.

– I want to be in your story!

I can fend off all this grunting for as long as the Three Roses is open, for as long as it's warm and dry. Better to suffocate than to freeze. Semmelweis-Märrie takes me under her wing.

– She's not all there, but she's harmless.

She sends us away just after midnight. She shows no mercy. Once she let Klunker-Lupo spend the night behind the bar. We beat the hell out of him the next day – right in his ugly mug, wants something better, ha! He knows his way around, not with us!

Since then Klunker-Lupo dutifully stands with us under the kiosk roofs and only works evenings for Semmelweis-Märrie, which we've graciously allowed him to do in return for several rounds of beer. My latest training regime is called 'night shortening'. For this, you have to sleep during the day, in a bus shelter or on the bog in the Caritas shelter. It rains under my bridge. I'll go mouldy if I spend any more time there. So I lump together with the others, even though they're the last resort, the last hole. But *I* have my calling, *they* have their beer.

– Tell us a story, they mumble, and, missing their mouths, they tip beer down their fronts in yellow, stinking streams. I steal a receipt book from Semmelweis-Märrie, it's no skin off my nose.

My upper thigh and arm hurt for a few days, then everything was healed. The charges against persons unknown weren't recorded, a criminal investigation was instigated against me. The delegation at the secondary school refused me admission: no more places available, according to the letter. Father once more held court at the school: his daughter had been subjected to harsh treatment, she was attacked.

– Proof?

– The scar on her arm.

– I don't see any scar. Unfortunately we can't do anything, Herr Doktor. In any case, university places are reserved primarily for workers' children.

– Why?

– For the sake of historical fairness.

Father had lost his power. Katka Lorenz had an idea. Katka was the only one who believed me. After listening to what had happened to me, she demanded that the crime be solved and the offenders be charged and punished. These phrases made me anxious. I already practically believed that I'd been mistaken, that I'd cut myself in a fit of madness, and had dreamed the rest. Katka came over and wanted to get to the bottom of it. Crouched under the veranda, the black spiders as witnesses, Katka wrote a letter to Leibnitz district council. She described what had happened, asked for help.

– As easy as that, she said.

I envied Katka for her maturity and courage. I'd never had words like these at my disposal, such foggy, exhausting concepts that surely meant something. Katka was cheerful and energetic while she helped me, and summoned up a whole heap of scorn against our teachers and the other students. Weeks passed. Katka didn't receive a reply.

She swore she'd go higher. The holidays arrived and at the beginning of the new school year Katka was missing. Transferred to another school, they said. Another time they said she was allowed to go to secondary school so she could study at university. Workers' children preferred. I searched the entire city for Katka. In her home I stumbled into the middle of a party – mother, mother's boyfriend, siblings – they sat in the splendid jumble of their own disorder, clutter and mirth... Didn't I know where Katka was?

– Get lost, you stuck-up tart. She's not here!

I asked at the secondary school.

– Katka Lorenz? Not here.

– She has, my father explained, gone to Timbuktu, like your mother and that actor.

– Where's Timbuktu?

I didn't understand anything any more. Everyone had left me, one after the other. No one showed me how things should be and where *I* should go. No one took me with them. We moved out of the villa into a one-bedroom flat in the spring. Frau Schramm was the next to leave me. The only thing she left behind was the green kneeling cushion covered in wax cloth.

– Your father's having a tough time of it. Take care of him, Ehlchen.

Father sold the bulky wooden furniture, the piano, the carpets. People Father called *criminals* moved into the villa. I wanted to know what they looked like, but a corrugated-iron fence was put up around the property, blocking the view. Sometimes I saw men going in and out, businessmen or something.

Father spent most of his time at the clinic. He was researching a new varicose vein operation technique, worked twelve hours a day, sometimes longer. Now and again he slept at the clinic until his next shift. The neighbours gossiped that he was having an affair with the night nurse. I'd come home from school and be all on my own. I didn't want to go to discos, or stand around giggling with the other girls. Fashion didn't interest me and I found the magazines smuggled over from the West and passed around among the girls boring. I missed Katka and in the evening, before I fell asleep, I had dream-like visions where I composed violin concertos. Sometimes my body went through a violent, prickly pain like the highest note of a violin. My time had come.

The worst was the fog. It enveloped me in civics lessons. It wrapped itself around my head, constricted my thoughts and dreams. I was always tired, incapable of following any lesson. Only in the evenings did my head clear when it filled with sound and relaxation. I listened to every violin concerto, any concerto, that I could find on the radio. I would take up a ruler and a pencil – and draw the bow effortlessly over the instrument in front of the mirror. C sharp! F sharp! D sharp!

I finished tenth grade with a Four. The 'I' was still there in the register, red and ominous. Lazy and woolly-minded, read the form tutor's report about me. Not unintelligent, but…

The only apprenticeship offer I received was as a mechanical engineer. When I showed my father the offer, he was furious. He chanted the words *mechanical engineer* like you might say *leech* or *tapeworm*. I shrugged my shoulders.

– So what? I'll become a me-cha-ni-cal en-gi-neer. I *have* to become *something*.

– Shame upon shame! Father commented, then he went back to his varicose veins and the night nurse.

The Red Cross distributes heavy lace-up boots from what has remained of the National People's Army stock. I pick out a pair to get through the first snow, along with grey woollen socks, fleece underclothes, a fur-lined Russian hat with ear flaps. I hang around the chip stall, Inge's Kiosk, in full gear, my colleagues fill themselves with grog, hardly anyone sleeps under the bridges any more, barely anyone knows a place to go. Atze steals some cigarettes and gets himself a couple of nights in the cells. Jail's good for those who don't booze. The Three Roses is good for the others, but only till midnight. Then horror and dismay set in. I'm writing less and less each day. Numb fingers, a dry cough, the Russian hat presses in around my head. Fog everywhere and the threat of awakening. Anything but that, anything but the fear of seeing myself.

On the afternoon of 18 December a metallic-brown four-door Opel pulls up in front of Inge's Kiosk. Two women emerge. One is in a fur-trimmed lilac leather coat, white stirrup trousers, her aubergine-blue hair in a severe bowl cut, rouge on her cheeks and chin, clinking earrings. The other is dressed alternatively in black, large silver rings on all ten fingers, lilac nail varnish. Noppe goggles, gets down on one knee and warbles:

– One screw with you two and I'll die happy!

Smiling politely, the ladies unveil their teeth, come closer. They are aiming for me. They've identified me as the only *woman* among all these mud figures. And this is what they have to say:

– May we interview you?

Noppe:

– *What* do you want?

– I beg your pardon, but you are a woman, aren't you?

– Yes, I say.

– We're from the magazine *Mammilia*, Cologne and Hamburg. We're writing a piece about women in need. This is Eva, I'm Isolde. May we also take your picture?

The leather-coated Eva rubs her hands together to signify the cold and discomfort, directing me, while Isolde, click-clack, shoots one photo after another. They invite me for breakfast in the café of the local hotel. Leibnitz's only hotel is almost empty. And when I enter in my Russian hat and soldier's boots, greasy hair and my skin grey like asphalt, the snotty hotel boy is ready to throw me out. But Eva and Isolde from Cologne and Hamburg have other ideas. They make way for me. Their throats spew Chanel No. 5, the lilac leather coat is proffered for taking and the silver signet rings say: *No buts!* I'm given coffee and cake, toast for eight marks fifty, another coffee and more cake. I can have anything in the hotel café, and it's as warm as a fairy tale. Eva and Isolde lean a little away from me, then I notice why: the warmth is reacting with my skin, melting the protective layer of sweat, releasing fumes, gases, miasma. I sniff inside my woollen jumper.

– Need the loo.

I wash myself, wherever possible, in the gleaming mirror-tiled bathroom of the Leibnitz Hotel. The awakening is getting closer. Just don't panic, Gabriela. The good soap foams up. In the mirror I see my grey mask, hang my hair under the running tap, rub soap in it, wash out the slop until it's black and fragrant, then dry it – cheeks red and healthy: I'm awakening. What do you look like, Gabriela? What are you wearing? Where did this Russian hat come from? Everything on you stinks. You've dropped into the last hole.

The big international women's magazine *Mammilia* awaits you in the café. They want an interview with you and to take your photo. I should have washed my jumper too, the filthy jeans should go straight in the bin, and these boots! I'm overheating from the confusion. Lilac Eva comes looking for me: I don't have to be embarrassed, people know too little about the women in need in the East. But this article in *Mammilia* will send a message. 'Women Having to Huddle under Kiosk Roofs' will be the title.

What was my name?

– Gabriela von Haßlau.

– Fffon?

– Noble Anhaltinian stock.

– Tell us more, tell us everything.

The awakening. The total awakening. I pull packing paper, a torn poster, a semicircle of a cherry-stained bag, toilet paper, all of it filled with writing in pencil, from the plastic bag containing my possessions.

– This is my story.

– You write?

– My life.

Eva writes on her notepad: Woman writes.

– Tell us more!

I show them the first part of my story. A great moment.

– We'll publish it! rejoices Isolde. Snap, snap, put your hat back on. Don't smile for goodness' sake, look how you always look: aggrieved, dejected, tortured. Yes, that's great. And now like you're freezing. Yes! Yes! And now like you're hungry. Brutally hungry, great!

Awakening. Awakening. I'm hot. I take off my jumper.

– What are you doing? Actually, this underwear's perfect! Dreadful, yes! Yes! That's going to be a great photo! Roll up the sleeves. Do you have any tattoos? No? Pity, but wait a minute, what's that? Did somebody hurt you?

– I'm a Binka.

– Say again?

They take pictures of the round scar tissue. Eva manically takes notes.

– What a story! We'll make you famous!

Coffee, cake, more toast.

– Eat, Frau von Haßlau.

Aglow from the joy of discovery, the women forget their disgust, pat the stack of papers.

– *Mammilia* will drag you out of the gutter!

Is my name Binka? Is my name Ehlchen? Perhaps my name is Gabriela? Gabriela von Haßlau? I'm full, clean, doing well. I still have nothing, but I'm already walking a little differently on the cobbles of Leibnitz. Elegantly, proudly, in heavy black soldiers' boots. Everything's going to change. That evening in the Three Roses I buy a round. Then another and another. And one for Klunker-Lupo behind the bar too, and one for Semmelweis-Märrie. The glass washer has a drink. Ha-ha, drinks, slurps, boozes.

– He's breaking my glasses, shouts Semmelweis-Märrie.

– Another round. Today *I'm* buying.

– She been shitting gold or what?

– She's bonkers, that's what she is.

Klunker-Lupo knocks back the twenty-third beer… and collapses. His head with the hole hits the bar, blood everywhere. Even I'm back in the fog.

– Now *you* can wash up, barks Semmelweis-Märrie after Klunker-Lupo's carried off in an ambulance.

I stand behind the bar of the Three Roses, washing glasses. Are you awake or are you dreaming? It can't be real.

I flew away during 10a's leavers' ball. Father had bought me a gauzy silver dress for the occasion.

– It's time to become a lady, Gabriela.

The advantage of the dress: the director's hour-long speech ran off of it like liquid soap.

– As of this day, declared the director, we have entered our socialist reality, one of productivity, a life of peace, of solidarity, of challenges. He spoke of our abilities: we were a steadfast group of people ready for anything. And the time has come, the director knew to add, to prepare ourselves against those hostile towards us.

The first Sekt of my life. Father stuck to apple juice. He stayed for half an hour. His face had darkened during the speech. What made me tired made him angry. He went to work, and I danced in my silver dress with Grumert-Thomas and and and… then I jumped out of the second-floor window, danced across the schoolyard, down the street, my certificate fluttering in the wind, a piece of bumph.

That was the summer I started to write. Short, sassy stories, high jinks by naughty girls, seduction fantasies. Father read them after work, his moustache twitching with amusement.

– What's the matter with you?

– Assignment.

– School's finished.

– That's why.

Father checked if I had a fever. The surgeon's fine-fingered hand stroked my forehead and cheek. Ether, iodine, varicosis. I thought Father had got smaller, the white giant had shrunk, the once-black moustache quivered in a faded grey. Ever since we stopped living in the villa everything had become much smaller. I spent the whole summer in my room. I dropped out of time, woozy, endlessly tired, weak.

– We're going to the Baltic Sea, Father decided.

The sea didn't revive me in the slightest. Father went on long solitary walks on the beach, cursing and grumbling to himself. I asked him about the night nurse and he cut me off.

– That doesn't concern you.

On 1 September my apprenticeship as a mechanical engineer began at the Leibnitz Industrial Plant. It was called the I-Plant for short and specialized in the manufacture of hydraulic pumps and milling machine parts. The first day of the apprenticeship comprised 100 lots of five kilograms of iron. They put me in blue overalls, wrapped a headscarf around my hair, gave me sturdy black leather shoes. The air was stagnant in the machinery hall. I was pushed into position. *So you know your place.* My training began. My mentor, Kulisch, led me to a stack of iron plates, pressed a file in my hand, assigned me to a machinist's vice.

– File every edge at a thirty-degree angle, round them off, let me know when you're done.

Every iron plate weighed five kilograms, 'women's weight', Kulisch called it. I heaved the plate up from the pallet, pressed it against the bib of my overalls, took three steps to the vice, clamped it in the lathe chuck. Too loose – the plate slipped, I pulled my feet back just in time, the part flew clanging like a bell to the floor. The other operatives at their machines turned their oily faces in my direction, grinning. Start again, Gabriela, watch what you're doing. Clamp it securely, not too high, not too deep. Position the file and go. The tool grated across the metal. I froze when it made this sound, shook like a dog. Get on with it! Ten minutes and I still hadn't managed a single plate. Each plate had eight sides to file! Don't tilt the file like that. How stupid are you, girl? I got a dusting of fine filings all over me. After working on three plates I had blisters on my hands and pains in my shoulders and back. Another ninety-seven to go, Gabriela, then a thirty-minute lunch break. The file got hot and dull. I forgot to file one of the sides on a plate, it had to be fetched back. You'll be filing for the next fortnight! By lunchtime I'd finished a measly six plates. Filings and oil had sunk deep into my palms and when the machine was turned off there was a ringing like an alarm in my skull. There was a lump of paste made from sand and almond clay to wash with. I rubbed my hands together with it like the others did – they were red, swollen and raw. It couldn't be done.

Kulisch:

– *Who* do you think you are?

Five kilograms of iron, heave up, press to bib, clamp, screw down, file, position, up and down, thirty-degree angle, release vice, hold the plate tightly, turn the plate, retighten, file, up down up down, only fucking's better, rotate, change, take off plate, set aside, check with bare fingertips, five kilograms of iron, heave up, clamp, turn it the other way, nose wipe, iron stinks, bad filing cuts into flesh, five kilograms is women's weight, arms like a heavyweight, the screech of drilling, shriek of milling, screech of grinding, file by hand, up down, the stack of plates shrinks, the other grows, filing needs technique not strength, but where do you get it from without keeling over, round file, flat file, riffler, what's better, stopping is better, throw everything away, *Four* according to the certificate, weak pass, so keep filing, five kilograms, don't look around, don't look up, after eight hours I don't know who I am. My name is Gabriela von Haßlau. My father is chief medical officer, top vascular surgeon at the Leibnitz clinic. I for Intelligentsia, I for I-Plant. I sink into hot bathwater, try to feel my body: This is *you*, Gabriela von Haßlau. Close my eyes, my mind keeps filing, file, file, metal on metal, water, soft Ba-Du-San bubble bath. Take the plunge, bathe in Ba-Du-San. This is your life, stupid Binka. Six o'clock in the morning at the work-bench. And again, 100 times five kilograms. Where are the others? There's not much difference between a violin concerto in A minor and an iron plate in need of filing. That's what I told myself, the crust of work softened from my skin, the world seemed bearable bathing in Ba-Du-San. The next day the 100 iron plates I had filed awaited me. So you know your place. Pay attention. This is an electric drilling machine. We'll drill here and here. First put the puncher in position here, put the mallet on it – ping! First run. Make 200 small, cone-shaped inden-tations, every plate gets two holes. Ping! The puncher jumps off the plate onto the floor. Clink. Pull feet back at the right moment. We call that a drill chuck. Repeat after me, Gabriela, *drill chuck*! And this is how we open and close it. The drill chuck key fell to the floor, the part fell to the floor, I fell to the floor, all my strength. You're useless! Kulisch clamped a plate in the machine, main switch on, mind out, Gabriela. He slowly led the drill bit downwards, he had to meet the punch point exactly otherwise the drill would break, drill in slowly, bring it up straight away, dab the whole thing with drilling fluid otherwise it'll smoke, back down again, slowly, moderate strength, you'll know when you're through.

This machine was a monster. Within ten minutes two drill bits had broken on me, I'd put four holes *next* to the markings. Shavings and filings fell all around me: small, greasy iron filings, thin spirals of aluminium, round curly

87

ones made of blue steel, colourful flickering artworks, waste, dirt. I made filings too: dull ones that broke when touched. Shavings to sweep up, shavings soup made of drilling liquid, dust and blood. I saw black and collapsed. Before I fainted, Kulisch thundered: Turn the machine off! And: They shouldn't send us females as apprentices. After I fainted there was theory. We apprentices were taught about occupational safety by means of a slide-show presentation. Strong footwear, bulky like military boots, otherwise – see slide of crushed feet. No jewellery, no rings at work, otherwise – see torn-off fingers, ears, garrotted throats. Hair always kept under a hat or headscarf, otherwise – see worker scalped by drilling machine. The realistic photos brought on my second fainting episode. I spent the rest of the day in the I-Plant's women's relaxation room, where a medic treated me with camomile tea.

On my third day, after I was led to the milling machine – which Kulisch more precisely called a horizontal shaping machine – I didn't even make it to the second work process. Actually, I clamped one of the plates I'd already filed and drilled into the machine, then everything swam in front of my eyes. I gave it some juice, the milling cutter began to turn, the iron plate slid forward, everything was measured incorrectly – the cutting edge crunched against the plate, jammed, a bang, the machine came to a halt.

– In the shit again! Kulisch bellowed.

I avoided his grasp and ran out of the hall. Down the dark stairs, dark-red brick, brown tiles, a hundred doors, a hundred halls, no exit. Green arrows, warehouses, tool store, first hall, second, third, insulation, pumping hall, paint shop, no exit, off limits, caution: explosion hazard, no light, a placard newspaper listing Best Workers, mildew, fug, emergency exit. I, Gabriela von Haßlau, trainee in the first year of an apprenticeship as a mechanical engineer, stood outside the back exit of the Leibnitz I-Plant in overalls and protective footwear. This was where the canal flowed by. Goldenrod and plants that looked like huge sticks of rhubarb rose stiffly from the bank. The canal was brown here. Whatever the I-Plant released into it was thinned out a couple of kilometres along by the coloured waste from the wool-dyeing factory. I stood on one of the large concrete pipes protruding like the rectal opening of a mighty beast and stared at the thick brew of waste water. Concentrated drill liquid, shavings, blood, along with kitchen waste and shit. Everything into the murmuring canal running along its stony river bed. Then sunshine. The factory roared behind me. I didn't want to do it any more. I won't cooperate. Then he got me. Kulisch grabbed me from behind by my braces, I slipped away, slid down the bank to the canal. Kulisch, uncertain of his prey, slid down behind me.

– What's wrong, Gabriela?

– Don't touch me!

Kulisch threatened to make me stand to attention in front of the assembled workforce. But *of course* I could trust *him*. He wasn't a monster. I tore myself away, rammed my right knee into his hip. My mentor toppled and fell into the canal. He climbed out on the other bank, stinking, dripping. I ran as fast as I could. I was grabbed just before the wool-dyeing factory. Two men linked arms with me.

– Good afternoon. Name's Queck, said one, and the other said:

– Never mind.

They drove me home.

– Get changed, then come with us.

I did what they said without protesting, took leave of my room, took leave of the world. The men put me in a black Volga. Queck sat in the back next to me and nudged me in the ribs.

– So pretty and already so badly behaved.

He laughed and wiped his bald head.

He had a pot belly like Pittiplatsch, the goblin from the television show, and wore a gold woman's wrist-watch. I decided not to say a word and to switch off my fear just like the drilling machine. Who were these men anyway? We drove through the whole of Leibnitz. Queck gabbled about his time as an apprentice: he learned cook-ing, ha-ha, nothing much, he got where I was coming from, ha-ha, although he could still cook, ha-ha. Can tell by looking at you, said the other one.

Semmelweis-Märrie is satisfied.

– You've got a screw loose, but it'll do for washing up.

Semmelweis-Märrie pays me 800 a month, I don't know what to do with this windfall. Everything's happening all at once: the magazine *Mammilia*, my story serialized, and now – a job. A secure, well-paid job. I clean glasses like I've got a life to make up for. For three days, four. Then I'm fed up with it. Get an infected thumbnail and backache. The Three Roses is busier every day, the usual characters jostle about, gloomy grunting men... some of them just stand around, don't order anything, simply warming themselves. When it's late in the evening I have to chuck them all out; it's not a refuge, it's a pub. I turn them out of the door into the snow. They grope their way into the crisp white, each to their den, some hole in the Leibnitz earth, to come back here the next evening to thaw, to spit frost, tiredness, thirst in my face, because *I've* made it, I'm out of the shit.

Now I sleep in the broom cupboard. Semmelweis-Märrie reluctantly allows it.

– You need to look for another place, slut, she says, moving ladders and mop buckets to one side to make room for me. The cupboard reeks, I can't get to sleep the first night because of the strong stench of Ajax and liquid soap, firelighters and detergent. But it's warm and private. If only you knew!

The next day Chief Inspector Paffrath is standing in the Three Roses, leaning his fat belly against the bar and demanding to speak with Gabriela von Haßlau.

– That's me.

The Three Roses holds its breath. A cop at this time can't mean anything good. Everyone's on edge. Semmelweis-Märrie's cherry-red mouth warbles:

– Fräulein von Haßlau is officially employed here. Everything's above board with the tax office, Inspector.

Paffrath knows his audience well, and couldn't care less about practical jokes, but there's one he has to pursue. He places something on the bar, colourful, beautiful, a magazine. The cover photo shows a grey-faced woman in a Russian hat, large dark circles retouched under her eyes, something like pockmarks on her cheeks and forehead, badly healed cuts. Headline in fat yellow letters: 'Leibnitz Poetess Scrapes by on the Canal'. A feature spread and the first part of my life story.

– Is that *you*? Paffrath asks.

The Three Roses gawp like they've never gawped before.

– The Binka's cuckoo, we knew it.

– Yes, that's me.

Look at that: the cop's smiling! A potful of lard smirking, his fish lips tilting upwards.

– Don't you feel ashamed, putting something like that out there?

– What's that supposed to mean?

The Three Roses piss themselves laughing. Beer sloshes over lips and bellies. Paffrath changes the leg he's standing on and asks whether we could speak, just the two of us… It's ultimately a city matter and he didn't come here to make accusations, but rather…

– Rather what?

Semmelweis-Märrie allows me to leave.

– Take the cop with you and don't go thinking you're better than us!

– Don't you have somewhere to live?

– Yes, here.

– In the bar?

– Yes.

– So the article's true, is it?

We walk through the snow in silence. Past the closed-down factories, black houses, across the Green Bridge and the Sunday Bridge. Further on, through vacant streets, across squares, wondrous glitter, the once-in-a-century winter. Just before my bridge.

– This is where I used to live.

The policeman laughs.

– Now you're exaggerating!

We remain standing there, leaning over the railings. The canal swirls beneath us, snow hangs over the embankment, great white bales of magical sugar. The little moss house is snowed under.

– Do you know who lives there?

– Grit for the roads. Paffrath lights a cigarette, gives me one too. We smoke in silence.

– Why are you shaking your head, Fräulein von Haßlau?

– Because it's not true.

– You made up the story.

– No.

I'm standing and chatting on my bridge with a cop.

– It's strange, but do you know what?

– We're going down to the station?

– No. Paffrath's gloved fingers roll up the latest issue of *Mammilia* and he smacks it against the bridge railings.

– You look completely different from the photo.

I close my eyes, let the winter snow settle. And let the chief inspector stand, smoke, jabber on next to me. Wake up and know: it's time to keep writing.

– Where do you want to go now?

– Back to the Three Roses.

– Can I see you again tomorrow?

– A cop tells, he doesn't ask.

– Off duty, he says.

– What do you have in mind?

– Goodnight, Paffrath says, shakes hands like a good little dog, goes on his way.

Queck and his driver took me to an apartment in Leibnitz's newly developed Fritz Heppelt quarter, named after the anti-fascist resistance fighter. Ground floor, two tiny rooms, overheated. The door to one of the rooms is closed. They placed me in the armchair of a scuffed, teddy-bear-amber three-piece suite in the other room.

94

The armchair was on wheels and beneath it the imitation parquet flooring was worn from being run over. Queck fell onto the sofa opposite me, breathing heavily. The Pittiplatsch pot belly sagged into the upholstery.

– Huh! whistled out of him.

Wall-mounted shelves with books and bric-a-brac: a clay-coloured deer, thick Bohemian glassware, the Berlin TV tower made of plastic. Right at the top was a dusty, stringless violin. I gazed at it in irritation.

– Played by a faaaamous virtuosa, Pot Belly bragged, waved the driver over and whispered imploringly: Make it a strong one, Manfred.

Manfred disappeared into the tiny kitchen, the coffee machine started gurgling, and Queck proceeded with the preamble, building trust: I shouldn't worry, shouldn't be afraid. Many had sat here before me, I must know that our republic offers many opportunities, and anyway, and this is the main thing, this is why I'm sitting in this lovely chair: it's come to their attention that I write stories, assignments.

I flinched.

– How do you know that?

Queck gave a friendly wave of his hand. Manfred served the coffee in yellow waffle-patterned stoneware cups, ripped open a packet of Hansa butter biscuits, arranged them on a plate. He sat down next to Queck, nodded encouragingly and told us to help ourselves. Manfred was a head taller than Queck, with a smooth, childlike face. I wondered if he had ever grown a beard. I was sweating and found it hard to listen to Queck's speech.

– We know, Gabriela, that a lot has happened to you. An unfortunate story, as it were.

– Filing isn't a lot of fun.

– We can understand that. But we mean the other things: your father, your mother, the actor Samuel, your late Uncle Schorsch, not forgetting Katka Lorenz, your friend, am I right? And also not forgetting the strange incident where you cut your arm.

– I was attacked.

– You already told us. But we don't want to talk about that.

Queck slurped his coffee and bit into a bone-dry biscuit. Sweat glistened on his fat face, while Manfred listened sitting very still, nodding every now and then.

– Oh, and not forgetting, ah, the thing with the mentor... well, um, ha-ha, ha-ha...

Queck wiped a biscuit crumb and with it my past from the table. I added triumphantly, because I had something to add:

– Not forgetting Frau Popiol, my teacher.

Queck looked puzzled. Manfred shrugged.

– Don't know her.

Faint nausea came over me like hunger pangs. The violin lay on the top shelf looking like a dachshund. What had happened?

Manfred opened the window. Outside, children jumped between sheets and duvet covers drying in the yard.

– A once-in-a-century summer! Queck sighed.

We'd been sitting in the amber three-piece suite for two hours already. My thoughts strayed, the laundry brought in a fresh breeze, Manfred tapped the face of Queck's woman's watch.

– Let's get to the point, Gabriela.

I was half asleep as Queck laboriously lifted himself up off the sofa. I wasn't sure how long he'd been talking. I wanted to go home. I was free. I never had to operate a machine ever again.

– Never again, Queck confirmed.

They loaded me into the Volga and drove me a different way home from the one we'd taken before. Father went the same evening: he had to travel to a surgical conference for a couple of days. He kissed me, stroked my hair. He left me money.

– You're old enough, Gabriela.

Four weeks later I received a postcard of the Bamberg Horseman. 'There was nothing I could do' was written on it. I ripped up the card. There was no one I could show it to. With the green kneeling cushion under my knees, I scooted across the bathroom tiles and the linoleum in the kitchen. Scrubbed, wiped, polished away the last of Father's particles. I took the curtains from the windows, filled the bath with water, soaked them. The dark brew spurred me on: tablecloths, towels, rugs – everything underwent a thorough clean. I pounded, rinsed, wrung until I fell into a deep sleep, my heart racing.

The next day Queck woke me up. He knew about the Bamberg Horseman.

The cultural department of the Leibnitz Industrial Plant. My first area of operations. No more filings, no stink of metal – a desk with a yellow Sprela top, a telephone, folders. I didn't know what I was entrusted with, sat about and didn't do anything at first. Three long days of doing nothing: show up in the morning, eat lunch in the canteen, finish at four o'clock. My two colleagues in the department ignored me. They didn't say a word to me. They sat with their backs to me, rummaging through paperwork and processing employees' holiday requests. Barely a word was exchanged between the two of them either. They would give each other the odd telephone number at best and said words like *bed occupancy* and *trade union*. After three days Queck picked me up from the factory:

– What do you have to show us?

– Nothing.

Queck's comfy pot belly tensed menacingly.

– You've got real talent. My God, Gabriela, you would be doing us a huge favour.

I did him a favour, followed both of my colleagues from the cultural department to the bathroom. There they would puff on long Duett cigarettes and in whispers

I heard the words *bed occupancy* and *trade union* again. In spite of my best efforts, I couldn't understand anything more than that. I retreated to the women's relaxation room, which was empty most of the time, and which Queck had had allocated as *my* space. I wrote a piece about *bed occupancy* and *trade unions*, wove observations like whispering and Duett cigarettes into my prose and bemoaned the secret smoking. After composing these lines I lay down to rest, slept. The week wasn't yet over and I was fired from the industrial plant for a second time. Queck and Manfred drove me to the open-air restaurant at the racetrack, bought me beer, tried to convince me of something or other. They put me between the both of them and walked me through Schiller Park, round and round the goldfish pond. Gabriela, Gabriela, you can write, we know you can. They chauffeured me to this place and that, over bridges, past restaurants, they stopped at the Kabinett Mühle, Leibnitz's artists' cellar. They knew of it, gave me instructions. I listened to them, forgot immediately – awakening was the worst! Queck stroked his belly.

– Quatsch-Platsch! he laughed, and Manfred:

– You're no longer called Gabriela, you're called…

They let me go. They stood in front of my door. I waited for a postcard of the Bamberg Horseman. A payslip arrived. What for? I thought.

The curtains, towels, carpets had been washed. I'd done nothing since then. Am I called Binka? Am I called

Ehlchen? The neighbours gossiped behind my back. I wrote and wrote. Crazy, unreal stories. Full of errors, full of pride. Queck came in, gave me time, gave me encouragement. What for? You'll see. No one gets lost. Who am I supposed to find again? Anything but awakening. Awakening was the worst.

I have to suspend all glass washing for a week. My infected thumbnail hurts, the nail bed festers. Semmelweis-Märrie froths in anger:

– It's not a castle, Your Majesty!

I wash glasses one-handedly. The regulars breathe out winter, only Rampen-Paul's cigarette gives off a glimmer of warmth. They all cluster around it, frozen or beaten blue, in thick tattered coats, with five o'clock shadows. Leibnitz has spat out its people. The canal freezes at the edges and Semmelweis-Märrie keeps the Three Roses open half an hour longer than she has to. She gets off at half past one in the morning, stomps home to her heated flat, while I clean dirt and slush from the barroom and turn out Noppe; open the windows so the fug can escape into the bitterly cold night, a cloud of bad breath.

Chief Inspector Paffrath is on night duty. He looks in when the last guest is out of sight. I unlock the back door and the Inspector says:

– Evenin'.

Semmelweis-Märrie forbids me to put more coal on the fire at night. Paffrath says it's a disgrace. Me behind the bar, Paffrath alone in the barroom, he orders a tea.

– People are talking about you.

– Time I got out of here.

– Yeah.

Silence. The hot tea warms the whole room. Paffrath sucks on a cigarette. He's taken off his hat and his thin hair stands up on end, quivering.

– Baby hair, I say, giggle, chuckle, holding my stomach, which aches from laughter. Paffrath tousles the silky quiff.

– Yeah, baby hair, but there's a man underneath!

Our laughter fills the Three Roses. I come out from behind the bar, pointlessly adjust the two standing tables, clean the windowsills. Paffrath wants to know how my writing's coming along. He's been following the series in *Mammilia*. I give him a light for the cigarette.

– It's a secret!

– Fine by me.

Paffrath smooths down the baby hair, puts his hat back on, taps the visor.

– I'll come by again tomorrow.

Kabinett Mühle. When I entered my name was Binka. All I knew was that I was invited, cordially, to this groundbreaking exhibition of work by Leibnitz artists. Go there, Queck said, read what you've written. Everyone will be presenting their work. My heart beat right up to my eyelids with pride and fear. I turned the thin, grey pieces of paper with my story written on in pencil in my hands, practised reading aloud in front of the mirror, and twisted a golden hairband into my hair. That was *me*. An aspiring poet. I forgot what Queck wanted from me the moment I descended the stairs into Kabinett Mühle.

Throng. Semi-gloom. Strangers laughing. And: Hello! Most people were dressed in creased black fabric, nettle cloth and linen. They had ribbons tied around their foreheads, silver rings and jewellery made from adder stones and mussel shells. They wore their hair long or hedgehog-short, wide baggy shirts and skin-tight trousers, black nail varnish and hand-woven shawls. I felt ashamed in my ordinary corduroy trousers and conservative Dederon blouse. So ashamed that I wanted to leave, but Queck's goblin voice was breathing down my neck:

– Last chance, girl.

Throng. I was shunted around. *My* performance was to be at nine o'clock.

– Hello! I greeted people I didn't know.

– Hello, who are you?

– Gabriela von Haßlau.

– Are you in tonight's programme?

I fled to the wall. How was I supposed to survive here, in all this laughter, all this whispering, all this desire to show something new and different? Grope along the wall and act like you belong here. Vodka and cola. Maybe it'll help. There were things on display everywhere: tables of pottery, bookstalls, art galleries. I admired the charm of it. Music. Four young musicians appeared on the stage built in the middle of the cellar and played jazz. The figures in black danced to jaunty jazz and gloomy blues. I got carried away: I knew the blues, a wonderful distant memory. I shook my arms and legs in time to the music like the others. I slowly started to awaken. Hello! someone called, and I said: Hello! Danced, jumped, *I scream! You scream! Everybody likes ice cream!* Throng. Now it's the singer. Tall, hair as red as field poppies.

– Frau Popiol! I shouted, forcing my way through the ever-growing crowd. Frau Popiol! The blues came over of me like a force. The cellar sang it. Everyone joined hands, spotlight on the red hair. This is your last chance, Gabriela. I'm called Binka. Blues. I'm falling too. Where to? Wherever you want. The blues ended, Frau Popiol disappeared. The guests were welcomed by Samuel the actor. He bounded onto the stage, threw out his arms to catch the applause.

– Samuel!

The crowd swallowed me up. Applauded. Great things were expected. Samuel sang and played guitar. The cellar held its breath. Now *those* were songs. Rousing, strange and intimate, sung ardently. What was I supposed to do with them? I should do something! I looked around for help. Plumes of smoke from Karo cigarettes, expectant faces, every now and then a head craned up. Applause. All for Samuel. I had to speak to him. I fought my way through the audience.

– Do you remember me?

– Gabriela! Samuel was in a hurry.

– Where's Mother?

– You haven't heard?

– Tell me.

The crowd absorbed the actor, pulled him into the maelstrom. *I scream! You scream!* the jazz band sang.

– And now, the Skunks, the workers' cabaret of the Leibnitz Industrial Plant!

The Skunks performed sketches. Everyone sat on the floor in delight, they'd seen them before, knew what to expect. I could hear the sound of slamming doors coming from somewhere. I was dissolving with sweat. You're on soon. After the next *I scream* they'll be listening to *you*! My mouth was dry with agitation and my eyes burned from the Karo smoke. What did Queck say? I'm sick, I thought for a moment: my brain wasn't connecting up anything any more, of what had happened, what I wrote and what I was doing now. I'd forgotten, completely, what this was all about. I heard the name Gabriela von Haßlau.

– Come on, girl.

It was Frau Popiol who shoved me onto the stage. The cellar fell silent. My teeth chattered as I reached for the thin grey paper in my trouser pocket. The spotlight blasted me in the eyes. Dust, dancing smoke, whirling, swirling bliss. I read what I had written. Quietly at first, as if spoken through cotton wool, then my resounding, defiant voice filled the room. They clapped when I had finished. I stepped into the dark abyss of the audience.

Throng. *I scream.* A few people gathered around me: Where did I get *these* ideas from? Fabulous, how brave I was! Hot, bashful joy. Is *this* what Queck wanted? Did he hide from me that he knew I was sick? What else did he know? I jazzed my way through my glee. I could barely tell who I was dancing with in the dark cellar, nothing mattered, everything was new and vast. I hoped in vain to find Frau Popiol, and just once from deep within the haze I heard the words: Kurt is dead.

I jazzed my way into my new life and promised to keep having *these* ideas and to be brave. I wasn't sure what I had been courageous about. *Can't buy me love!* the band sang. Karo ruled the Kabinett Mühle, another vodka and cola to know life a little better. Dancing. It doesn't matter where happiness comes from, it has to fall into your arms and make you forget. I breathed into unfamiliar hair. Tight embrace, *Can't buy me love,* hands roam over a body, down a strong back concealed by a black creased dress.

– You read very well, the dancer said.

– Oh, I said.

The music cut out. I looked into Katka's face. How beautiful she'd become! Not really slim, but a miracle of gaiety. We kissed, locked in an embrace. She lifted me into the air – she had the strength of a crane, whirling me around. Suddenly she said:

– Let's get out of here.

– And go where?

– Wherever you want.

Hand in hand, we walked through the city. We had years to talk about.

– I moved out right after school finished, Katka boasted. She had become a painter. Hadn't I seen her pictures in the Kabinett Mühle? I hadn't. I felt ashamed not to have paid attention to anything other than myself, to have taken pleasure only in my own happy state.

– Can't believe you've become a poet! Katka scoffed.

I started. Now I really was one! A poet. I was happy. Now I knew where I belonged.

– I had to file and drill iron plates, can you imagine!

– *What* did you do?

We sniggered our way through the city, recounted our scandals and misdeeds, every little experience. We were free and in high spirits.

– But how do you make a living, Ehlchen?

We danced by the canal. At night the brewery let its juices flow into it, hops and malt and foam flakes churned, and we were drunk. Somewhere, at mine or at hers or somewhere else, we fell asleep, dog tired.

I woke up at noon, naked, on an unfamiliar mattress.

– Katka! There was no one in the flat apart from me. Katka had disappeared. Did I dream it? I wondered, looking down at myself: blue bruises on my chest and legs, the pain almost pleasant. My time had come. But what had I done? And where? I tumbled through the chaos of bedclothes and washing, knotted curtains, misplaced carpets, countless items of clothing belonging to me, or to someone else? I knocked over coffee cups, cold coffee grounds dribbled onto the floor, clinking glasses rolled away from me. I was at home. In my flat. Katka had been here too. I saw the front door standing open, broken open. Fell over my mess, banged my knees. They were standing behind me.

– Put something on, Queck said.

Manfred, his driver, looked away grinning. I did what was asked of me. Anything but awakening, I pleaded, trying to clear up.

– Leave that! yapped Queck.

I let it all fall to the floor and asked where my friend Katka was. Manfred shut the door behind us. Just as I sat down in the black Volga I felt sick. I threw open the car door, got out, puked up the sour remains of vodka and cola in front of the bonnet. Queck let me sleep leaning against his pot belly. The car pulled away.

Atze and Noppe stormed the broom cupboard.

– She's not kosher! Snobby cunt! Smug bitch!

They came in through the window, beat me out of my sleep.

– Made yourself a warm bed in here, and Paul's already shuffled off and I'm about to do the same.

Noppe stabs a knife into the detergent canister. The soapy stream hits me in the face.

– Get out, fucking get out!

Atze slits open the box of snow grit, throws the sharp dirt everywhere, Fisherman-Kurt and Chicken-Beppo climb in through the window, crack! The broom and the mop snap, ha! I get a thrashing, soap, dust, violent coughing. The rats cleave a way into the barroom.

– Nice and warm in here!

More and more of them come. Ha! And all on the house! The beer taps hiss. They stick their muzzles under them, wild stinking animals, and get their fill. Someone lets off the fire extinguisher and sprays foam into the broom cupboard, the vinegar cleaning fluid explodes. Police! Police! The Three Roses plug up my mouth, the bar's falling apart, it's cosy here, boys! And even more appear: the overnight guests of the Green Bridge and the Sunday Bridge come in from the once-in-a-century winter, stopping off at mine on the way. One shouts:

– She's a Binka!

They seize me, rip out my hair.

– She's not one of us! She's got a villa, she's just sounding us out!

With all my belongings under my arm, I crawl outside through the throng of rampaging tramps. The winter has polished Leibnitz as smooth as ice. Fleeing, I skid onwards through the early morning streets. Police! They're smashing up the Three Roses!

Chief Inspector Paffrath leads the operation. Three green police vans. Atze, Noppe and whatever the rest of them are called climb in without putting up a fight.

Once upon a time there were three roses. Paffrath takes me down to the station too.

– Why lower yourself to this level, Fräulein von Haßlau?

– Not my fault.

– Done your research?

– What have I done?

Paffrath doesn't believe me. He lifts the plastic bag with two fingers, the shelter blanket, my possessions, and he throws them in the corner.

– But you're an artist.

– I'm sick, Chief Inspector.

– Oh boy, you're giving me quite a night of it.

I now own nothing except Paffrath's chaperonage. Six o'clock, end of shift. In his car he asks:

– Where should I *really* take you?

I don't know. So tired not a single response comes to mind. He takes me to his place. Ninth floor of a new apartment block. My knees start shaking while I'm still in the passenger seat. Cop! I think. The building smells of cigars and the rubbish chute. We walk down a corridor that's at least 100 metres long.

– I always do a little sprint at the start, Paffrath jokes.

He leads me into his flat. A bulky brown three-piece suite neatly fills the only room. I'm so tired I could collapse.

– I'll run you a bath, then sleep, and tomorrow we'll see.

Sleeping in a foam forest of conifers, floating deep in dreams. Paffrath wakes me with a shower of cold water.

– You could drown and not even notice.

He gives me a towel, his gaze signalling restraint. Wrapped in the towel, I consider what to do with the pile of filthy clothes that I've worn for the last few months and that are now lying pitifully in the corner of the bathroom. I'm embarrassed, but Paffrath says briskly:

– Let's get rid of those!

Valiantly biting back disgust, he gathers up the rest of me, carries it 100 metres along the corridor and throws it down the rubbish chute. Comes back, shows me a place on the sofa, beds himself down on a mattress on the floor. The first night without the cold, and the smell of soap. There's only the hum of pain in my infected fingernail. The Chief Inspector snores in his dreams, loud little puff sounds slip out of his mouth. He turns over onto his side with a grunt. I look at his baby hair, sticking to his head thin and fine, and I fall asleep.

*

Drunk from sleep, I climb out of the black Volga.

– Let's take a little break, shall we?

Queck bends his legs, while Manfred suppresses a groan as he stretches the small of his back. We were in the countryside, a forest and a lake. The day was clear and enticing.

– Breathe it in, Gabriela!

– Wermsdorf, enthused Queck, the VEB Inland Fishery! They've always got something put aside for us. Let's go and see.

We walked around the small grey lake and entered a barracks.

– Our fishermen! Queck introduced a group of men sitting around a table having breakfast. The men, their countenances as cold as fish, followed our entrance sceptically.

– Breakfast! demanded Queck, and rubbed his thighs in anticipation.

Without saying a word, the men prepared a table for their guests, fetched plates of smoked fish, eel and carp. Queck asked for Schillerlocken – Schiller, ha-ha, his locks, ha-ha, it's actually pieces of smoked dog shark, and *Oh, the shark has pretty teeth, dear*, and can be found in the Wermsdorf Lake.

The fishermen's faces remained an icy grey, as if they had to listen to these stupid jokes every day.

– Time to get to work, one of them said. The rest followed him outside, while Queck and his driver Manfred picked at the Schiller curls. Two fingers lifted the little golden rolls from the plate, the neck bent backwards, the curls dangled, gently swaying over the open mouth, the tongue caught drops of oil, then the lips snapped shut. I bravely drank coffee. Smoked fish would have made me throw up all over again, and anyway, what was I doing here? Queck wiped the grease from his mouth, nudged Manfred with the wink of an eye.

– Let's do it, OK?

Manfred grinned, leaned back in his chair. Queck invited me on a boat trip. Outside, in the fresh air, I felt better. I followed the goblin belly. I had to follow him. After all, who else would know what was wrong with me? Manfred got into the boat first, steadied it. As Queck plopped down onto the deck, it rocked violently. They put me in the middle, Queck sitting opposite me on the wooden bench. Manfred grabbed the oars. We cast off. After the first strokes I awoke. Suddenly I saw who I was sitting in the boat with, knew what had happened the night before, where I'd been, who I'd seen. The game had been called. Manfred steered the boat, Queck squinted against the morning sun. I pressed my hands between my knees. Awakening was awful – this clarity was bringing on a headache, and every second of pain brought me closer to the realization: *not that.* Now to you, Gabriela. Queck picked a bit of fish out of his teeth. I sat rigidly.

– We're waiting for your assignment.

– Why?

– We were clear about that.

– About what?

– Listen, we're not here to joke around.

– Please take me home.

– What are we supposed to make of that?

– I can't do this any more.

– She can't do it any more. Were we so wrong about you?

Queck's pot belly sank between his spread-out legs. I could see the threads of the grey Malimo trousers so precisely, could see this man in his full nakedness so clearly, that I was filled with horror. I'd already forgotten what he'd said. But Manfred's oar strokes reminded me: we're going to make you disappear, like Mother, like Father, like Frau Popiol, like Katka, like...

– Where's my friend Katka?

The question interrupted Queck's sentence. Queck's friendliness disappeared.

– You've disappointed us, Gabriela.

In the middle of the lake Manfred stopped rowing. The boat circled around its axis. Midday sun. Queck's bald head shone like the skin of a smoked fish. I imagined Schiller locks growing out of his skull.

– You know what happens if someone betrays our trust.

– There's still one more chance.

– Make it quick! Manfred's milky face grimaced impatiently. No one's around.

I looked for the Wermsdorf fishermen in vain. I was alone with Queck and his driver.

– *One* more chance, Queck repeated.

I was awake like never before. The boat swayed.

– What are you doing?

Pot Belly turned pale. The oar slipped out of the driver's hand.

– Damn it, watch out!

Queck's fingers grabbed at my knees for help. I stood up abruptly, balanced myself. The oar tilted upwards in my hands – the long side met Manfred's head, the driver tipped out of the boat. Queck cooeed for help. I jumped to the port side. The goblin fell over, his legs wedged between the middle seats. I dragged him out by his shirt collar, the oar circled before his eyes, slipped out my hands, splashed into the lake, where Manfred was drifting motionlessly among the farmed fish. Queck was as heavy as a sack of potatoes. His shrill cries for help irritated me. I jumped into the water, hung onto the edge of the boat, while the fatso rolled starboard and the boat listed and tipped over together with him. I swam away as Pot Belly floundered in the lake, gurgling. Swam with great, peaceful strokes to the bank. No one around. I climbed out of the water and left without looking back.

Waking up in an unfamiliar room. On a sofa under a clean, cosy blanket. Where am I? And who? Poet, homeless, unemployed. The clock says ten past six in the evening. I'm alone. A note on the table from Paffrath: 'Wait for me.' In the kitchen, sausage and bread laid out on a plate. Men's things draped over the arm of the chair. I should put them on for the time being. But I'll greet Paffrath with nothing on. Him in his uniform! 'Naked Woman Welcomes Policeman'. Headline in *Mammilia*. *That*'s it! *Quite* the stunt! I have to bring my story to an end, devise something explosive to get me out of the last hole. Semmelweis-Märrie will have to wash the glasses herself today. Or not at all. Because no one will come. Dosser raid under my authority. They'll all be locked up, nice and warm. Or maybe released straight away, back into the winter. Rummage through Paffrath's apartment: men's socks, cigarettes, old newspapers. And a pad of fine white paper. I sit at the table with this in front of me. Anhaltinian nobility. Fffon Haßlau. Poet. Naked in front of a cop. Who'll believe it? The readers of *Mammilia* await the next part of the story. The part about the nobility is good. My father was an eminent doctor. We had that already. It has to end differently, in a completely unexpected way.

When I got home from the boat party the flat had been sealed up. I hitchhiked to Mecklenburg. A derelict barn, covered in moss right up to the gabled roof, offered me shelter. I found a job in the cattle shed of a small farming cooperative near Crivitz. My tasks were: cart dung, scrape dung from udders, keep dung separate from feed. Get up at four every morning, head to the shed reeling from lack of sleep. The creatures roared. Their swollen udders were sore and resistant to medication. Two of the milkers at the cooperative milked the twenty cows by hand before stoppering the teats with the milking machine's cups. The milkers, still half asleep, would squat on the stool, had no age, no face. Barked in my direction:

– The teats have to be clean!

I washed the udders with mineral water, cut off any gummed-up hair on the cows' stomachs, cleaned their snotty noses with muslin. The animals objected, their tails hit me around the ears. Straw was scarce and was spread over the encrusted faeces only twice a year before the state inspection. They were fed with pellets that stank of fish, and a mix of cabbage and turnips. The animals chomped on it for milk and meat, for the milkers, for the cooperative. The milk, thin and watery, shot into the hoses of the milking machine. Cowpats slapped onto the slats. I swung the five-pointed fork, stuck it into the sludge, lifted the steaming excrement, loaded it into the wheelbarrow. A third man came, threw pellets into the feeding troughs, poured water on top of them, woke up the milkers. I stood up to my knees in manure. Maria and Agathe snorted on the back of my neck, Suse stepped on my boots, Anna unleashed a jet of piss from above. I carted the muck outside, where it was thinned out with water and tipped onto the fields. And that's how it went, day in day out. After four weeks of back-breaking work I had three days off; I slept through them in deep unconsciousness. At the village pub, the cattle farmers' dialect reigned supreme. They wouldn't let me sit with them. I would just toddle off to bed. One day all twenty of the cows in the shed were dead. The corpses lay in the muck as if sedated. *Schit!* the farmers said. I left Crivitz in the night, fled across the paddocks in the direction of Teterow. Had had enough of working in cattle sheds. I made it through by stealing and working as a labourer. Katka's training came in handy. If they caught me, I knew the game would be up. There were no more last chances. I got work with a farmer by the name of Rieck. My tasks were to peel potatoes and clean carrots ready to hand to the farmer's wife. Then Farmer Wilken, the neighbour, entered the Riecks' kitchen one evening in his heavy work boots.

– The streets in Teterow are full of people. They're marching through the town. It's all happening!

– What is?

– I don't know, but I reckon we should join them!

Farmer Rieck said:

– What's that got to do with me?

Farmer's wife:

– Horst, you have to!

Wilken left a streak of dirt behind in the kitchen, grumbling as he went. I scrubbed the tiles, the potatoes, grated carrots and apples till my fingers bled.

– You say something?

The farmer's wife, a blue apron around her protruding hips, eyed me suspiciously. I wanted to ask what was happening, what was going on in Teterow or wherever it was, but the question stuck in my throat. I'd got used to never saying anything to anyone, not even my name, and if I did introduce myself I called myself Binka or Katka or Maria Elke Popiol.

– Pisspot! The farmer's wife poked the farmer.

– Wilken's talking sense.

I left the Riecks' farm in the night, headed for Teterow. Standing on the outskirts, I saw thousands of people making their way through the streets of the town. The sight swam before my eyes. They won't be looking for you any more, I thought to myself. Your time has come.

I hitchhiked my way back to Leibnitz. Told every driver my name: Gabriela von Haßlau.

– From the West?

– No.

– And where do you come from?

– Anhaltinian nobility.

– Either you're telling the truth or I'm driving you straight to the madhouse.

No one believed me. I searched for those I still hoped to find: Katka, Samuel, Frau Popiol. I found nobody.

No one that knew me. What's more, they were after me. The whole city knew my name. After a few days of restless searching, and a few nights of sleeping at the Christian hospice, I handed myself in at the police station.

– Gabriela von Haßlau.

– Identification card?

– Don't have one.

– We've got more pressing problems at the moment. Gabriela von Haßlau. We get all sorts here...

They kept me in overnight, reported me to the social welfare office, held their noses whenever they came near me.

– Get *that* out of here! complained one of the uniforms. That's all we need, the top dossers round our necks.

They drove me to the psychiatric ward.

– Schizo, the driver explained, delivering me like a package.

– I'm the daughter of Chief Medical Officer Ernst von Haßlau.

– Let's start off by lying down very calmly.

– I'm the daughter of Chief Medical Officer Ernst von Haßlau.

– We don't know of any Chief Medical Officer Ernst von Haßlau. How about you give us your real name?

– Gabriela von Haßlau.

– And do we know your year of birth?

– Well, I do.

– Would we say this pencil is yellow or red?

– *I'm* not crazy.

– We're all going to stay very calm. What have we been up to recently?

– I've been hitchhiking. You?

After three hours of anamnesis, the psychiatric ward decided to release me. I stood out in the street. Someone was banging on the windows inside the mental hospital behind me. Kurt had it good, I thought to myself, he didn't have to go through the revolution. Then I had to find a place to sleep, sign up at the welfare office and the homeless shelter. The summer was hot and dry, a once-in-a-century summer.

Paffrath closes the door to the apartment.

– I've bought you some clothes, he says. Takes off his uniform, takes off his shoes, stretches his stiff toes. He brings me two plastic bags emblazoned with Henry & Moritz.

– Put these on.

The bags stay where they are on the floor. I approach the Chief Inspector, my hands slip under the olive-yellow police shirt, it's warm, a throbbing tone like a swallowed watch signals signs of life.

– Don't you like them? Paffrath gestures to the bags of clothes.

– I like everything you do.

Paffrath's hand moves nervously to his nose. He scratches it. The shirt slides out of his trousers, I gather it up to his chest. White stomach, a hairy chest and back, my hands patrol the area.

– Ah, Paffrath says.

He carries me to the sofa. I lie on my stomach. He kneels in front of my face. *No!* I want to shout. Paffrath's smooth hand grasps me underneath my hair, lifts my head. White legs, chest, stomach, white, all white. I recognize every little hair on his body.

– *Mygoodgirlmydarlingmybeauty.*

No! Paffrath lays my head back against the cushions. I turn over, pull my knees up to my chest, my arms embrace my thighs and calves. I make myself small, invisible. Paffrath lends a hand, raises my backside and shows me what he wants in depth. I roll on my side, stay lying there. Inert.

– Your first time?

Bewildered, Paffrath rises from the sofa, smiles, goes out into the hallway, brings the bags in.

– Trousers or a skirt?

Something must have happened. The story stops short. It wasn't bad. Wasn't pleasant either. Paffrath puts a bright, floral skirt on my naked stomach. Then he makes himself a sandwich in the kitchen. Wine to toast the day. A dark, snowy afternoon. He sits in the armchair draped in his dressing gown. He puts both his feet up on the edge of the sofa. His eyes twinkle like a tomcat's. I lie there in silence. How warm it is. Paffrath eats his bread and sausage, raises his wine glass, lights a cigarette.

I throw the skirt on the floor, unroll myself, look Paffrath in the face. The twinkle flares up green and hot, then Paffrath closes his eyes and it goes out.

Subscribe

Discover the best of contemporary European literature: subscribe to Peirene Press and receive a world-class novella from us three times a year, direct to your door. The books are sent out six weeks before they are available in bookshops and online.

Your subscription will allow us to plan ahead with confidence and help us to continue to introduce English readers to the joy of new foreign literature for many years to come.

'A class act.' GUARDIAN

'Two-hour books to be devoured in a single sitting: literary cinema for those fatigued by film.'

TIMES LITERARY SUPPLEMENT

A one year subscription costs £35 (3 books, free p&p for UK)

Please sign up via our online shop at www.peirenepress.com/shop

Peirene's Series

COMING-OF-AGE: TOWARDS IDENTITY

NO 13
The Dead Lake by Hamid Ismailov
Translated from the Russian by Andrew Bromfield
'Immense poetic power.' GUARDIAN

NO 14
The Blue Room by Hanne Ørstavik
Translated from the Norwegian by Deborah Dawkin
'Shrewd and psychologically adroit.' LANCASHIRE
EVENING POST

NO 15
Under the Tripoli Sky by Kamal Ben Hameda
Translated from the French by Adriana Hunter
'It is excellent.' SUNDAY TIMES

....
CHANCE ENCOUNTER: MEETING THE OTHER

NO 16
White Hunger by Aki Ollikainen
Translated from the Finnish by Emily Jeremiah and Fleur Jeremiah
'A tale of epic substance.' LOS ANGELES REVIEW OF BOOKS

NO 17
Reader for Hire by Raymond Jean
Translated from the French by Adriana Hunter
'A book that will make you want to read more books.'
COSMOPOLITAN

NO 18
The Looking-Glass Sisters by Gøhril Gabrielsen
Translated from the Norwegian by John Irons
*'The real strength of this book lies in the way so much
is withheld.'* DAILY MAIL

FAIRY TALE: END OF INNOCENCE

NO 19
The Man I Became by Peter Verhelst
Translated from the Dutch by David Colmer
'A haunting, apocalyptic novella.' GUARDIAN

NO 20
Her Father's Daughter by Marie Sizun
Translated from the French by Adriana Hunter
'Affectingly restrained... Impressive.' THE SUNDAY TIMES

NO 21
The Empress and the Cake by Linda Stift
Translated from the Austrian German by Jamie Bulloch
'Composed with the logic of a bad dream.' GUARDIAN

....
NEW IN 2017
EAST AND WEST: LOOKING BOTH WAYS

NO 22
The Last Summer by Ricarda Huch
Translated from the German by Jamie Bulloch
'She is the First Lady of Germany. No, she is probably the First Lady of Europe.' THOMAS MANN

NO 23
The Orange Grove by Larry Tremblay
Translated from the French by Sheila Fischman
'A little jewel, finely chiselled.' ELLE

NO 24
Dance by the Canal by Kerstin Hensel
Translated from the German by Jen Calleja
'30 years of East German history narrated with laconic irony.' DIE ZEIT

COUNTERPOINTS ARTS

Peirene Press is proud to support
Counterpoints Arts.

Counterpoints Arts is a charity that promotes the
creative arts by and about refugees and migrants
in the UK.

---

*'We are living in a time of human
displacement. We need bold and
imaginative interventions to help
us make sense of migration. And
who better to do this than artists
who are engaging with this issue.'*

ALMIR KOLDZIC AND ÁINE O'BRIEN, DIRECTORS, COUNTERPOINTS ARTS

By buying this book you are helping
Counterpoints Arts enhance the cultural
integration of refugees – a mission which will
surely change our society for the better.

Peirene will donate 50p from the sale of this
book to the charity.

www.counterpointsarts.org.uk